NO ONE HAD EVER TRIED TO ROB THE DIMMIT COUNTY BANK. . . . YET.

Sheriff Jim Ed Crow sat on the porch of his small, box-shaped office in the early morning heat, complaining of indigestion to his deputy, Tinker Warren. He noticed a dust cloud on the southern horizon. Squinting, he said, "Something's moving out there . . ."

Tinker watched the dust cloud a moment. "Comin' from the river. Appears they're in a hurry."

Crow felt the beginnings of concern. Anyone who hurried a horse through this heat had to have a good reason. Dust boiled from the distant brushland, swirling skyward. A voice inside warned the sheriff, a voice from his experience in the war. "Get those Winchesters," he said as his right hand fell to the butt of the Colt .44-.40 holstered against his leg.

"Bandidos," he whispered. The fear beginning to rise in his chest. A bank robbery could wipe out every business-man and rancher in Dimmit County.

Jim Ed Crow hoped he was wrong.

He knew he wasn't . . .

BORDER JUSTICE

FREDERIC BEAN

ZEBRA BOOKS
KENSINGTON PUBLISHING CORP.

ZEBRA BOOKS are published by

Kensington Publishing Corp.
850 Third Avenue
New York, NY 10022

Copyright © 1994 by Frederic Bean

Zebra and the Z logo Reg. U.S. Pat. & TM Off.

First Printing: September, 1994

Printed in the United States of America

Chapter 1

Carrizo Springs lay like a pale green emerald in the desert flats of South Texas, twenty miles above the Mexican border. It had been an oasis for weary, thirsty travelers since the first settlers came. Today seemed like any other summer day. Temperatures would hover near one hundred from noon until dusk. Local citizens sought the shade of thatched porches or the cool interior of adobe houses through most of the afternoon. Work was all but impossible outdoors in this unrelenting heat. Livestock in the surrounding dry brushland grazed only where slender mesquite leaves provided an escape from the sun. Even the hardy Spanish goats rested until temperatures cooled with the coming of dusk.

At the center of the village a pool of crystal water sat inside a grove of drooping willow trees and sturdy cottonwoods. The spring was the lifeblood of this tiny town, the only reason for its existence. Surrounding Carrizo Springs was some of the driest land in Texas, an unyielding desert as harsh as any in the north of Mexico. Like most of the rest of South Texas, roughly half the county's population was of Mexican descent.

Dimmit County was once said to be a lawless no-man's land, a haven for cattle thieves and men on the run. What law there was now came from the office of the county sheriff, a position held by a battle-scarred veteran of the Confederate Cavalry under General John Bell Hood. Jim Ed Crow had seen his share of the fighting, from Virginia and the Pennsylvania woods to the mountains of Tennessee. Though the war had been over for more than twenty years, he remembered it as if it were yesterday, and still dreamed about the bloodiest battles at night when he'd eaten too much chili pepper or habanero sauce. Today, after another sleepless night brought on by an extra helping of Rosa Mora's chili *rellenos* washed down with tequila, he sat on the porch of his small box-shaped office, whittling on a green mesquite stick, still complaining of indigestion to Tinker Warren, his twenty-two-year-old deputy.

"It's the reason most white folks die young in this part of Texas," Crow said knowingly, slicing more thin shavings to the floor of the porch, his leathery face wrinkled thoughtfully as though the observation required deep contemplation. "Mexican food is exactly what it says it is . . . food for Mexicans. A white man who eats it is asking for a dose of misery."

"There ain't much else to eat around here, Sheriff," Tinker replied. "Everything spoils in this godawful heat."

"If you ask me, Mexican food is spoiled when it's cooked. The claim could be made it's been ruined to start with."

"Then don't eat no more of it, Jim Ed." Tinker's solution sounded simple enough.

"I'd starve. Can't say which would be worse—being

poisoned by Rosa Mora, or just wasting away to nothing."

Tinker stared out at the brush. Heat waves danced above the cholla and mesquite. "You hear any more 'bout that trouble brewin' down in Mexico?" he asked.

Crow wagged his head. "Just that another revolution is building up. Mexicans stage revolutions all the time. Could be the food has something to do with it. A man with a bellyache is sure as hell more inclined to start a fight. I'll bet I woke up a hundred times last night. If I coulda gotten my hands around Rosa's neck, I swear I'd have strangled her."

"Word is, ol' Luis Zambrano is behind all the trouble down there," Tinker remembered. "Folks claim he's one mean *hombre*."

Crow sighed, thinking about the Wanted circulars on the wall of his office. "He's got a bad reputation and there's no denying it. I've heard it said he's one of the worst border bandits they've had in quite a spell down there. Wouldn't be no exaggeration, judging by the rewards being posted."

"We've been lucky he ain't shown up around here," Tinker said, his voice trailing off.

Crow eyed the bank down the street, knowing it would be a temptation should a revolutionary army need money. Davis Mercantile would also be a lure with its stock of guns and ammunition. "I don't figure they'll bother us. I might sure as hell be wrong, but Carrizo is probably too far above the border."

"Ain't but twenty miles, Jim Ed. Half a day's ride if a man's in enough of a hurry on a good horse."

Crow didn't particularly care to think about the possibility of a bandit raid. He and Tinker wouldn't stand much of a chance defending the bank and the store against a handful of *pistoleros*. "That's the driest twenty miles on earth," he said absently. "A man would have to be plumb crazy to ride a horse hard across it in the summertime. It'd kill the average animal. The gent would have to know what he's doing . . ."

Tinker nodded thoughtfully, still watching the brushland. "I sure wouldn't want to try it. There's at least a thousand rattlesnakes between here'n that river. A feller on foot would have to be real careful where he stepped."

Crow belched loudly and made a face. "Goddamn that Mora woman," he grumbled, "puttin' all that extra pepper in her stew pot. It's a wonder that cast iron don't have a hole eaten plumb through it by now. I swear by all that's holy I ain't never gonna eat another bite down at Rosa's place. She can poison the rest of you, but she's had her last shot at trying to kill me. If I could think of something to charge her with, I'd toss her in jail for a week or two. Disturbing the peace is what it is, fixing a man so he can't get a wink of sleep. I was damn sure disturbed all night last night."

Off in the distance a donkey brayed. The sound reminded Crow that he'd neglected to feed his dappled gray horse. "Time I fed ol' Dixie," he said, closing his pocket knife and dusting the mesquite shavings from his faded denims with a calloused hand. He got up slowly, passing a glance across the rooftops of town. It was past noon, and most everyone was taking the *siesta*.

His bright blue eyes hooded when his gaze wandered to the bank. If a large bandit gang tried to rob the Dimmit County Bank, or the mercantile, he and Tinker would have a time of it trying to stop them. In the ten years he had served as sheriff of Carrizo Springs, no one had ever tried to rob the bank. But with a war brewing down in Mexico, the possibility loomed larger. Armies needed money. And guns. Carrizo had some of both. Would the town's resources be too much of a temptation?

Pulling the brim of his sweat-stained hat over his eyes, he sighed and stepped off the porch into blast-furnace heat radiating off the pale caliche hardpan. "I'm gonna toss ol' Dixie a handful of oats," he said. "Meet you over at the cantina after a bit, if you think you can stand any more of Alfredo's tequila. Last night, I'd have sworn you aimed to drink this town plumb dry."

"Wasn't all that much, really," the deputy protested weakly, making a face. "It was Carmela's fault. When I get around that pretty gal, I just naturally get thirsty."

Crow smiled. "That's a whore's job, to sell whiskey."

Tinker looked down at his boots. "I sorta wish you wouldn't call her a whore, Jim Ed."

Crow's grin widened. "Wouldn't hardly seem right to call her a saint or a school teacher, Tinker. Fact is, she sells herself for money, in case you're ignorant of how she makes her living. Not that I think there's anything wrong with being a whore. It's the world's oldest profession."

"I reckon it sounds kinda hard, seein' as she's so young."

Crow was set to offer further argument when he noticed a dust cloud on the southern horizon. Squinting, he said, "Something's moving out there. Hard to say what it could be, but it's sure as hell kickin' up a bunch of dust."

Tinker watched the dust cloud a moment. "Comin' from the river. Appears they're in a hurry, whoever it is."

Crow felt the beginnings of concern. Anyone who hurried a horse through this heat had to have a good reason. Dust boiled from the distant brushland, swirling skyward.

He frowned. "To be on the safe side, step inside and fetch down our rifles."

Tinker made a turn for the office door, still looking at the cloud of caliche arising from the flats. "Wrong time of day for some fool to be in such a hurry," he said quietly, thinking out loud.

A voice spoke to Crow, a voice from his past warning him that trouble was on the way. "Get those Winchesters," he said as his right hand fell to the butt of the Colt .44-.40 holstered against his leg. There was something about the cloud that began to bother him. He drew his revolver and thumbed open the loading gate to inspect the cylinder briefly, satisfied when he glimpsed six brass-jacketed cartridges gleaming in the sun. When the gun was returned to its leather berth, he climbed the porch steps without taking his gaze from the horizon. Something was out there and he didn't like the looks of it.

Tinker went inside the office and unlocked the gun cabinet as Crow was remembering the last time there had been any trouble in Carrizo Springs. A gang of rustlers was holed up in the northwest end of Dimmit County for a time, two years back if he recalled correctly, holding a herd of stolen cattle on unfenced land along the Rio Grande. Word came by way of a drummer that a handful of unsavory types guarded the herd day and night. Crow and his youthful deputy rode out that way to nose around and found themselves in a running gun battle with five hard cases, until the outlaws pushed their cows across into Mexico. That was the end of it. The rustlers were never heard from again. Lawmen from Texas were powerless below the border. It was Mexico's problem after that. The border was the prime frustration for peace officers on this side of the river. Outlaws could jump the Rio Grande with the law in hot pursuit and they were free men.

The dust thickened. Crow watched it with growing apprehension. He could see tiny specks below the swirling cloud, and he knew horses and men were churning up the dust, moving toward Carrizo Springs in one hell of a hurry. No one in his right mind ran a horse in the middle of the day in this country. Something was wrong.

Tinker hurried out on the porch and handed him a Winchester model '73 with a badly scarred walnut stock. Crow had owned the gun for years; he trusted its sights. He levered a shell into the firing chamber and then gently lowered the hammer with his thumb while staring at the specks on the horizon. "I count eight or nine men," he said. "Could be more."

"They're all crazy," Tinker offered, balancing his rifle in one hand as he, too, studied the distant riders. "Any feller who runs a horse in this heat is downright loco."

Crow agreed silently, nodding. The little voice inside his head spoke louder now—bad news was headed his way. "Find a spot across the road where you've got some cover," he said. "Just a precaution, but I don't like the looks of this. Stay out of sight 'til we know what's going on." He glanced down the street. "Find a place where you can keep an eye on the front of the bank," he added softly.

Tinker left the porch to walk across the road. "You reckon it could be that Zambrano feller?" he asked, looking over his shoulder to examine Crow's face.

"Hard to say, son. It could be anybody. Keep your head down over yonder and don't take any chances. Remember this job don't pay much. No sense gettin' killed over twenty dollars a month."

Tinker hurried across the street, cradling his rifle, aim-

ing for a narrow alleyway between Davis Mercantile and
El Mercado Bustamante. No one was at the market this
time of day, and the windows across the front of the
mercantile were vacant. If bank robbers hit Carrizo
Springs now, fewer lives would be at risk if any shooting
started.

Crow's gaze drifted to the front of the bank. Harvey
Bascome's carriage was parked where it always was, in the
shade of a gnarled live oak tree at the southeast corner of
the faded brick building. Harvey would be inside now
going over his accounts with Harriet Sims, the bank's only
teller. Crow wondered if he should hurry over to warn
them of the possibility that a robbery could take place.

"No sense worrying them," he muttered under his
breath, staring at the specks again. "Not until I'm sure . . ."

He sauntered over to the office doorway and leaned
against the door frame, peering into the heat haze. A knot
was forming in his belly, and this time it had nothing to
do with Rosa Mora's spicy cooking.

Chapter 2

The distant rumble of hoofbeats grew louder. Crow squinted into the heat haze, counting the riders with his heart in his throat, his mouth gone dry. Fourteen men in dust-laden sombreros rode toward Carrizo Springs, and he knew now why they were coming. From a distance he could see the rifles they carried, bristling from the hands of men who would certainly know how to use them.

"Bandidos," he whispered, thinking about the bank, the money Harvey Bascome kept in his safe belonging to everyone in town. A bank robbery would wipe out every businessman and rancher in Dimmit County.

He trotted off the porch and broke into a run for the bank. Tinker saw him and edged away from the shadow between the two buildings, most of the color drained from his face.

"Them's bandits, ain't they?" Tinker shouted, his voice a little higher than usual.

"Stay down!" Crow answered without breaking stride, intent upon reaching the bank's front door quickly.

He hurried to the building and burst through the glass-paned doors. "Close the vault, Harvey!" he cried, glancing over his shoulder to the windows. "Mexican bandits at the edge of town!"

Harvey Bascome's fleshy face paled. He jumped up from the leather chair behind his desk and hurried to his office window. "Are you right sure, Sheriff?" he asked, peering through smudged glass to see the south side of town.

Before Crow could answer he heard a short gasp from the teller's cage. Harriet Sims clapped a liver-spotted hand over her mouth, briefly caught in a shaft of sunlight beaming through the front windows that made her silver hair sparkle as her knees gave way. She collapsed in a heap on the white tile floor, smashing her spectacles with a soft tinkle when they slid from her nose to the tiles beside her.

Harvey seemed not to notice Harriet's fall. "Where are they?" he asked. "I don't see a thing . . ."

Crow grew impatient with the banker's hesitation. "Close the safe!" he snapped. "And help Harriet. They'll be here any minute!"

Wheeling, he slammed the door and took off in a lumbering run for the mercantile, his heart beating wildly now. He and Tinker would soon be in a fight for their lives. Glancing south, he could see horsemen spread out over the brush-choked flats with dust curling from the heels of fast-moving mounts. The men were close enough for him to see the cartridge belts across their chests and the foamy white lather clinging to their horses. Fourteen heavily armed men made a terrifying sight bearing down on the outskirts of the city, reminding him of a lost war where brave men in gray faced overwhelming numbers in a fight they stood no chance to win.

Racing to the front of Davis Mercantile, he shoved

open the door and shouted to Buck Davis standing behind one of his glass-topped counters. "Bandits coming! Grab a shotgun and lend us a hand. Tell your wife to hide in the back room, and keep your head down when the shooting starts!"

He did not wait for the storekeeper's reply, or more questions of the type Harvey had asked. Time was running short. He made a turn for his office and ran as hard as he could for the front porch with the thunder of hoofbeats filling his ears. The Mexicans were galloping past the first goat herder's huts at the edge of town as he was crossing the road. Town dogs barked at the arrival of running horses. Somewhere close to the business district a voice shouted the alarm. Crow saw a cotton-clad boy run toward one of the adobe huts, pointing to the bandits just as Crow raced up the steps to his office.

He reached the door and stopped to catch his breath in the doorway. Across the road, Tinker peered around the corner of the market to watch the Mexicans gallop up Main Street. Pale yellow dust arose like a pall of smoke above the sweating horses, and now the drum of hooves was like the rumble of an approaching rainstorm.

They'll kill us all, Crow thought. Women and children could get caught in a cross fire. Storekeepers and goat herders stood no chance against experienced fighting men, armed with only a few shotguns, a rifle or two. He was sure he was about to witness a bloodbath in Carrizo Springs, the town he was sworn to protect. Against odds like these it was a one-sided fight, and he would be lucky to escape it with his life.

He moved behind the door frame and waited for the horsemen to come abreast of the office. Sweat dampened his hands as he gripped the stock of his rifle. His tongue was so dry he had difficulty swallowing. Above the din of pounding hooves, a strange ringing began in his ears.

His attention was drawn to a heavy Mexican riding at the front of the group. Below the drooping brim of a broad sombrero, a bearded face turned to watch both sides of the road. Crisscrossed bandoleers heavy with brass cartridges adorned the man's chest. A pair of gun belts encircled his thick waist. He carried a short-barreled shotgun in his left hand, resting the butt plate against his thigh. His black horse bore a layer of chalky dust and sweat as it carried him down the middle of Main Street.

Crow wondered if this was his first look at the infamous Mexican bandit, Luis Zambrano. Zambrano's bloody deeds were widely known on either side of the border. For almost a decade Zambrano had plundered ranches along the Rio Grande, always eluding efforts by the Texas Rangers and the Mexican army to capture him. It had long been rumored that Zambrano had paid informants among the *federales* who warned him of patrols sent to hunt him down in Mexico. His forays into Texas were swift, purposeful, always profitable in stolen livestock. Texas lawmen usually found only his tracks where he crossed the Rio Grande with his booty.

A movement across the road caught Crow's attention. Arturo Bustamante ran out on the porch of his market with an ancient double-barrel shotgun. Before Crow could shout a warning, a bandit riding at the front of the group drew his pistol; then things started to happen slowly, like in a horrible dream.

The bandit's pistol roared, echoing off storefronts, the sound trapped briefly between buildings. Arturo Bustamante was torn from his feet as though he embraced a mighty gust of wind. His shotgun flew from his hands.

Arms windmilling, his legs working furiously to keep him upright, he danced backward keeping time to some unheard melody. A splash of bright crimson splattered across the adobe behind him when a plug of his coal black hair exited from the back of his skull. His body was slammed into the wall, where it appeared frozen for a moment, invisibly skewered to the front of his store. One of the bandit's horses shied when it heard the gunshot. Arturo's weapon clattered to the ground while his torso was sliding down the pale adobe mud, his head leaving a sticky red smear in its path.

Tinker fired from the alleyway as Crow was bringing his rifle to his shoulder. The explosion from Tinker's Winchester sent horses plunging out of harm's way. A Mexican bandit swayed in the saddle when a .44 caliber slug passed through his chest; then the frantic lunge of his horse toppled him from his seat amid the sudden staccato of more pistols and rifles fired by bandits caught in the melee. Guns popped and cracked up and down Main Street as Crow steadied his aim on the leader of the gang. Speeding lead whined through the air; a bullet whacked dully into the front of the sheriff's office just as Crow was pulling the trigger.

The Winchester kicked into his shoulder. For an instant he was deafened by the roar from his own gun. Rocked back a half step, blinking to clear his eyes of burning gunpowder, he saw the first wounded Mexican fall beneath the horses' hooves. Crow worked the ejection lever as rapidly as he could. A spent shell casing flew past his face; yet his target remained aboard the black horse, and he knew he had missed badly when he saw a puff of dust arise from the adobe wall across the street.

A window at the front of Davis Mercantile shattered,

sending fragments of glass inward with a crash. Sunlit
shards scattered over the ground below the opening as
more gunfire erupted in the street. Somewhere, a woman
screamed. Crow turned his rifle sights on a bandit aboard
a plunging sorrel. The horse reared, forefeet pawing air.
He nudged the trigger when his aim steadied on the
Mexican's torso. The sharp report of his gun made him
wince, once again deafened by the noise so close to his
ear.

The bandit lost his sombrero when his body twisted out
of the saddle. His rifle fell. The sorrel bounded away from
the explosion, leaving its rider in midair for an instant.
Then the Mexican tumbled to the ground and landed on
his back disjointedly, booted feet delayed by the angle of
his fall until they, too, dropped lifelessly on the hardpan.
Crow ejected the empty shell, his hearing slowly returning. Guns thundered all around him, and the whine of
bullets drew him farther behind the door frame.

The concussion of a shotgun blast drowned out the
chatter of rifles and pistols. Crow watched as Buck Davis,
the front of his white storekeeper's apron cut to bloody
shreds, staggered through the half-open door of his store
holding his stomach. His knees gave way, and he knelt a
few yards from the opening at the edge of the boardwalk
as though he meant to pray. Blood poured from countless
tiny pellet holes in his chest and belly, spilling over the
wooden sidewalk. He swayed, his face twisted into a mask
of pain; then he pitched forward and toppled onto the
caliche road beside a hitchrail.

A ball of molten lead thudded into the clapboard above
Crow's head, and he ducked reflexively. Men and horses
dashed past the front of the office. Guns roared and
banged up and down the street. He saw horsemen charg-

ing toward the bank in a cloud of dust, and he knew there
was no way to stop them now.

Tinker fired from the alley. A bay horse whickered and
went down, tossing its rider over its head. The horse
landed on its chest, legs flailing. The bandit disappeared
into the dust churned up by the animal's flying hooves
before Crow could get the Mexican in his sights.

A shotgun thundered in front of the bank, accompanied by the sound of breaking glass. Windows across the
front of the building convulsed amid the roar. Harvey
Bascome's chestnut carriage horse broke its lead shank
and lunged away from the live oak tree with the buggy
teetering dangerously on two wheels behind it. Falling
glass rained down below the windowsills as a pair of
bandits jumped from their horses. The carriage bounced
and jolted down Main Street, leaving the ground when it
crossed wagon ruts on the way to the edge of town.

A wounded bandit tried to rise in the road across from
the market, coming to his hands and knees. Tinker fired.
The man collapsed immediately; then another shotgun
blast erupted in front of the bank, and before Crow
thought about the risks, he swung around the door frame
with the Winchester to his shoulder.

A muffled cry came from inside the bank. Closing his
mind to what the sound meant, he aimed for a bearded
Mexican near the bank's front door and squeezed the
trigger. The rifle jumped in his hands, barking so loudly
that every other noise around him was silenced. The
bandit's body jerked; he stumbled and dropped the shotgun he was aiming into the building. Crow watched him
slump to the caliche, failing to see the glint of sunlight off
a rifle barrel turning toward the sheriff's office.

A popping noise preceded the blow to his leg that

knocked him off his feet. He fell backward. His head slammed into the clapboard wall, and his vision was immediately surrounded by flashing pinpoints of light. White-hot pain shot through his left leg as he slid down to the porch floor with a thump. He let go of the rifle and groaned, reaching for the spot above his knee where the fiery pain began.

The leg of his denims was torn. He could feel blood coming from a gash across his thigh. When he tried to raise his head to inspect the wound, a wave of nausea gripped him. Bitter bile arose in his throat, and for a moment he was sure he would lose consciousness. His head dropped back to the boards. He gasped for breath, struggling to remain awake. More gunshots banged farther down the street. Much closer, a woman shrieked and began crying.

The muffled report of a shotgun blasted down at the bank, and again he tried to lift his head. He failed a second time when he was overcome by dizzy weakness. Another moan whispered from his tightly compressed lips despite his best efforts to contain the sound. The pain was spreading, moving down his leg in ever-increasing waves. A cold sweat formed on his face. He looked up at the porch roof beams. "I've got to get up," he groaned, gritting his teeth, grimmacing.

The rattle of gunfire died down to an occasional shot near the bank. Crow summoned all his strength and pushed himself up on one elbow. Blinking, trying to clear his head of cobwebs, he looked down the street.

Half a dozen riderless horses waited in front of the building, their reins held by three men in dusty sombreros. Behind glassless window openings, he could see more of the bandit gang near the teller's cage. "They've killed Harvey," he muttered softly, wincing when a fresh jolt of pain coursed down his damaged leg.

He then glanced across the road, pausing here and there when he came to a body. Buck Davis lay facedown in a pool of blood below the hitchrail, motionless. Arturo Bustamante was slumped against the front of his market, his head resting at the bottom of a red smear running down the adobe wall. A shirtless man lay beside the corner of the mercantile staring up at the sun, a blacksmith named Cotter Evans who somehow got caught in the deadly cross fire. The blacksmith's chest rose and fell, albeit slowly. Arturo and Buck were obviously dead.

The bodies of three bandits lay in the road between the office and the bank. A dead horse lay on its side in front of the market. Crow wondered about Tinker when he found the alleyway empty. Arturo Bustamante's wife knelt beside him, rocking back and forth with her hands pressed to her face, sobbing. Now that the gunfire had stopped he could hear barking dogs near the bandits' horses. A black cur nipped at the heels of a sweat-caked pinto gelding, snarling angrily.

Crow's arm trembled violently, and he eased himself back to the porch floor. His breathing grew more labored. Looking to the right, he saw the distance he needed to crawl to make it into the office, certain that he could not stand. Bracing himself for the pain, he rolled over carefully, dragging his injured leg to the best position for crawling. Sharp stabs of blinding pain accompanied every move he made. He began to crawl slowly toward the threshold. Sweat rolled into his eyes. His shirt was plastered to his damp skin. Moving forward only a few inches at a time, arms shaking with fatigue, he crawled to the opening without hearing another gunshot.

A shout down the street caused him to pause and find the source. What he saw made his blood run cold. The leader of the bandit gang marched Harvey Bascome out of the bank with a sawed-off shotgun at the base of Harvey's skull. Harvey was begging for his life in a high-pitched voice, pleading with the big Mexican not to kill him.

"Please don't shoot me!" Harvey cried.

The bandit laughed. While Harvey was in midstride, the shotgun went off. Harvey's head was torn from his neck, coming apart in hundreds of tiny pieces that flew in an equal number of directions away from the blast. Crow clamped his teeth and quickly closed his eyes before the pulpy remains of the banker's skull fell across the roadway. There was more laughter among the bandits; then Crow heard Harvey's body drop to the ground.

"The bastards," he hissed, crawling again, torn between hatred for the Mexican bandits and fear of what they would do to anyone else as they looted the bank and the mercantile. Raw-edged pain shooting down his leg took his mind off everything else until he was inside the office. He rested, catching his breath.

When he glanced up at the gun cabinet, he remembered his rifle. He lacked the strength to go back for it now. A twelve gauge shotgun and a box of shells rested in the rack, within reach. Pushing up on his hands, he crawled to the cabinet and took down the shotgun, then the carton of ammunition.

It required tremendous effort to turn around so that he had a vantage point at the bottom of the doorway. Sweating profusely, his senses numbed by searing pain, he opened the breech of the twelve gauge and loaded two shells. When he peered around the door frame, he saw bandits leaving the bank with canvas sacks of money. Despite his wish not to see it, his gaze wandered to the bloody stump of Harvey Bascome's neck and the blood-splattered ground around his body.

A commotion in front of the mercantile took his attention away from the looting at the bank. Sara Davis stood at the edge of the boardwalk with her palms pressed to her cheeks, shrieking when she saw her husband's remains lying in the road. A riderless horse passed between Crow and the woman, its reins trailing in the dust. A dark red blood stain covered the roan gelding's withers.

Crow searched the shadows between buildings for Tinker . . . there was no sign of his deputy anywhere. "I hope the boy didn't get shot," he said under his breath.

There was movement at the end of the street. Bandits were mounting their horses. Crow thumbed back the twin hammers on his shotgun, trying to ignore renewed pain in his thigh. When the Mexicans came past the sheriff's office, he would make them pay dearly. Then they would surely kill him, unless he could somehow kill them all.

Chapter 3

Ten hard-faced bandits rode slowly toward the mercantile, covering the street with their guns. Crow watched them approach with a queasy sickness twisting his stomach. During the war he had witnessed carnage of every description. Over time he'd grown more or less accustomed to it. But now, with bullet-torn bodies lying everywhere, some belonging to long-time friends, he was sickened by what he saw. His worst fears were being realized. The bank had been robbed, and now the bandits meant to loot the store and kill anyone who tried to prevent it.

Near a corner of the market, Cotter Evans stirred. The blacksmith rolled over on his side just as the Mexicans reached him. Crow watched, dumbfounded by the senselessness of it, as a bandit leaned out of his saddle to aim a pistol down at the ground where Cotter lay. For a fleeting moment the only sounds were the clatter of shod hooves and the anguished cries of Sara Davis kneeling beside the body of her husband. Then a gun exploded, spooking some of the bandits' horses. The wounded blacksmith stiffened and groaned. Again, Crow closed his eyes until the echo of the gunshot faded, wishing somehow this could all be part of a bad dream.

The gang rode abreast of the office, and none of the bandits appeared to notice Crow lying in the shadows behind the doorway. Bulky sacks of money hung from several of their saddles. Crow sighted along the twin shotgun barrels, bracing himself for the kick of the twelve gauge while slowly curling his finger around one of the triggers. This would be his best chance, perhaps his only chance, to catch the Mexicans tightly bunched together within shotgun range. As soon as he fired the first shot they would come gunning for him, yet his conscience wouldn't allow him to simply let them ride out of town unchallenged. He had to try to stop them if he could.

He squeezed the trigger, firing point-blank into the group when they halted in front of the mercantile. A terrific roar filled the confines of his small office. Crow's shoulder withstood a powerful blow when the twelve gauge went off, and in spite of the fact that he had prepared for it, he winced a little when the explosion hurt his ears. Beyond a billowy veil of gunsmoke rolling from the muzzle of his shotgun, he saw horses plunging and rearing. Angry shouts and the nickering of frightened animals followed the blast.

A lanky Mexican tumbled to the ground in front of the mercantile steps, spilled from the saddle when his horse bolted away. He landed head-first in a cloud of swirling dust. Another rider rolled off the rump of a rearing pinto, losing his sombrero and rifle before he fell. He struck the ground with his neck and shoulders just as a lunging horse bounded across his path. The unmistakable snap of a broken bone sounded; then the galloping sorrel stumbled and went down heavily, neck outstretched when it landed at the edge of the road.

Suddenly the caliche dust was so thick Crow couldn't find a target for his second shotgun charge. Two horses with empty saddles galloped south along Main Street. A gun exploded somewhere in the boiling dust. Wood splintered above Crow's head, and he quickly ducked into his shirt collar.

A horse and rider appeared, charging toward the sheriff's office. Crow aimed his shotgun and triggered off a hasty shot. He saw the bandit lift his arms just as his terrified dun gelding swerved underneath him. The Mexican pawed frantically at his chest and tumbled out of the saddle.

Guns blasted in unison from the middle of the road. Bullets whacked into the office wall. A slug passed through the doorway, shattering a lantern globe atop Crow's desk at the back of the room. Broken glass tinkled to the floor behind him; then the front window exploded with a mighty crash, and pieces of glass flew across the office like wind-driven snow.

As the last bits of windowpane fell to the floor, Crow was hurriedly reloading his shotgun, fingering red-hot, empty shells from the breech to make room for fresh charges. The scent of burning gunpowder assailed his nostrils. Someone shouted as he was closing the gun. Thumbing both hammers back, he only caught a glimpse of a running figure near the office steps before he was forced to aim quickly and fire.

A Mexican gunman swung his pistol toward Crow as he reached the edge of the porch. The shotgun belched fire and lead. A whistling load of buckshot struck the bandit's chest, accompanied by the tremendous clap of the twelve gauge. Speeding pellets at close range abruptly ended the gunman's run midway up the steps, knocking him backward while his feet were still trying to propel him higher. He seemed suspended in the air for a moment, boots churning as he was being swept away from the porch. Pieces of the bandit's clothing performed tiny spirals where buckshot ripped shreds from his shirt and pants. He fell, plummeting off the steps with a strangled cry caught in his throat. Bits of torn fabric fluttered slowly to the ground around him.

A galloping horse charged through the dust, aiming for the front of the office. The snap of a pistol shot sent Crow ducking for cover behind the door frame. A ball of lead thudded into the wall; then a rifle barked somewhere farther up the street. The bandit bearing down on Crow's firing position was knocked from his saddle, spinning with empty arms outstretched until he landed on his side in the road and skidded to a halt.

Crow had little chance to celebrate the fact that someone had come to his aid. He caught a glimpse of the bandit leader reining his horse in the direction of the office. Before Crow could bring his twelve gauge to bear, the big Mexican's shotgun discharged. A hail of lead pellets splattered into the weathered boards on either side of the doorway. Wood chips flew in all directions, becoming sawdust where the buckshot clustered. Pressed flat against the floor, Crow flinched and tried to make himself as small as possible, steadying his shotgun against the door frame. Spent shot rattled down on the porch as he was curling his finger around the remaining unfired trigger.

His shotgun boomed, driving the butt plate into his shoulder with enormous force as the black gelding swerved in the middle of the roadway. The shot went wide, sizzling across the street into the false front of Davis Mercantile without finding its mark. The bandit spurred out of range before Crow realized how badly he had missed.

Hoofbeats thundered down Main Street. The surviving members of the bandit gang raced south in an all-out run, and now all the guns fell silent. As the drumming of hooves faded away an eerie quiet came over Carrizo Springs. Crow dropped the empty shotgun to the floor to sleeve sweat from his eyes with a forearm. Dust began to settle around the porch. Now he could see the far side of the street . . . the boardwalk where Buck Davis had fallen and the prone form of Buck's wife lying in a spreading pool of red.

"No!" he whispered angrily. A stray bullet might have ended the woman's life . . . he prayed silently that the gunshot had not been one of his own when he'd been blinded by the dust.

Rising to his elbows, he inched around the door frame to peer south. The gang was riding hard away from town. With the danger past, his leg began to throb. When he looked over his shoulder, he saw a crimson stain on the floor.

Weakened by pain and blood loss, he collapsed on his chest when the effort to hold himself up left him drained and breathing hard. For a moment he lay there remembering the pitched battle, its grisly scenes, the noise and confusion.

"I'm alive," he said quietly, to himself. It was no small consolation. Badly outnumbered, he and a few townspeople had been able to drive the bandits out of Carrizo Springs. But not without paying a terrible price in lost lives. And now, those who survived the raid had no money.

He heard voices and raised his head. Here and there people hurried into the street to aid the wounded. Alfredo Garcia was the first to reach Sara Davis. Someone was running toward the bank, shouting for everyone to come outside now that the danger was over.

Straining, groaning softly, he managed to sit up, resting briefly against the wall to inspect his wound closely for the first time. An ugly gash lay inside the tear in his pants leg, an inch-deep slice across the skin and muscle of his thigh. Blood seeped from the wound, pooling on the floor below his knee. Every time he moved the leg, his pain worsened. He needed to stem the blood flow first; then he knew he had to face the gruesome task of counting the dead and wounded.

Someone was crying outside, a new voice added to the others across the road. Summoning what strength he had left, he used the office wall to climb to his feet. Although he was a bit unsteady at first, he discovered he could stand when he put some weight on his injured leg. Taking a deep breath, he hobbled across a floor littered with glass fragments to reach his desk and the old bandana he kept in a desk drawer. When the cloth was tied firmly around his wound, he turned for the door, for now ignoring the queasy feeling in the pit of his stomach and sharp pains down his leg each time he took a step.

He limped out on the porch to look for Tinker. His deputy had gone unaccounted for during the worst part of the battle, and it now troubled him greatly. When he looked up and down Main Street, there was no sign of the boy. Dreading what he would find in the alleyway where he last saw Tinker, he went down the steps very gingerly and started across the road, listening to Arturo Bustamante's wife wail tearfully beside the body of her husband.

He passed two dead bandits along the way, one whose face and chest had been pulverized by shotgun pellets, the other downed by a single bullet hole below his rib cage. Buzzing swarms of green-backed blowflies were already feasting on the drying blood, rising as a dark cloud when he passed by, then settling back to do their feeding. He merely glanced at the carcass of the bay horse on his way to the other side of the street. Farther to the north, the sorrel gelding with a broken foreleg struggled pitifully to stand, swinging its shattered hoof and cannon bone back and forth each time it attempted to rise. Crow promised himself that he would put the horse down humanely as soon as he learned Tinker's fate. He hated to watch an animal suffer and forced his attention elsewhere, where human suffering awaited him every place he looked.

The dead blacksmith's comely wife was weeping bitterly over the body when he limped to the mouth of the alley to look for Tinker. He felt some small relief when he found the alleyway empty. Now more of the town's frightened citizens were coming out to inspect the carnage along Main, faces he knew, friends and relatives of the deceased, the wounded. He saw Rosa Mora kneeling beside Sara Davis and stopped to inquire about Sara's condition before heading down to the bank.

"How is she?" he asked, examining the ashen face of the storekeeper's unconscious wife.

"It is her shoulder," Rosa answered, applying a bloody rag to a tear in the sleeve of Sara's pale green blouse. "She must have fainted . . ."

He merely nodded, for there was nothing much to be

said about a single tragedy when so many more awaited
him on the way to the bank. Resuming his painful limp,
he continued along the street, worrying about Tinker,
fearing the worst. The scent of blood was everywhere.
Heartbreaking sights and sounds surrounded him. Carrizo Springs would never be the same after today. He
knew no one would escape being scarred by the loss of
loved ones and friends.

When he drew near the headless body of Harvey Bascome, his stomach heaved before he could look away.
Gagging on bile, he forced his lame leg to move faster. To
the right of the bank's front doors, he saw a body stir. One
of the bandits was trying to crawl away from the building,
leaving a trail of blood across the caliche. A gaping hole
in the Mexican's back exposed flinty white rib bones and
torn muscle. The man was dying, yet still attempting to
make an escape by crawling on his belly.

A voice inside the bank startled him.

"Come quick, Jim Ed!" Tinker cried.

It was a tremendous relief to hear his deputy speak, to
learn he was alive. Crow turned for the doors and hobbled inside as quickly as he could.

He found Tinker seated on the floor beside the unconscious form of Harriet Sims. Tinker looked up as soon as
Crow entered the building.

"She ain't dead, Jim Ed, but I can't wake her up. She's
still breathin'. Can't find no sign of a wound . . ."

Crow sighed. "Maybe she just fainted. It's you I was
worried about. How the hell did you get down here without getting your head shot off?"

The deputy gave him a weak grin. "When I saw 'em
headed for the bank, I ran around behind the store so I'd
have a better angle. Soon as I fired off the first round, they

started blastin' away at the back of the market. Kept me pinned down until they got all the money. But I shot one of 'em. First man I ever killed, Sheriff. He's lyin' out front with a hole in his guts."

"He ain't dead just yet," Crow said, frowning. "The main thing is that you got out of this with your skin."

Tinker looked at the bandage around Crow's leg. "It don't appear you was quite so lucky."

"Only a flesh wound. I'll live. There's others who can't say the same. Buck and Arturo are dead. They shot Cotter Evans in the head . . ."

Tinker lost some of the color in his face, glancing outside. "Harvey Bascome ain't got a head, Sheriff. They blowed it plumb off his neck," he said in a hoarse whisper. "Worst thing I ever saw in my life, an' that's the gospel truth."

"I saw it," Crow replied sadly, remembering.

Tinker aimed a thumb over his shoulder. The bank vault stood open behind the teller's cage. Odd pieces of currency lay scattered over the white tiles. "They got all the money. Nothin' I could do to stop 'em."

"I know. You did the best you could. So did everybody else. Buck and Arturo. A few more. . . . I told Harvey to lock the safe. It don't appear he paid much attention."

"I reckon everybody here is flat broke now, includin' me," Tinker observed, after looking down at Harriet again.

Crow turned to the glassless window openings across the front of the bank. He took a deep breath of fresh air. "Some are worse than broke," he said in a faraway voice. "Hard for me to think of anything worse than bein' dead, Tinker." Now that the shooting had stopped, deep sorrow overwhelmed him. Four friends and neighbors had given up their lives trying to defend the town, and he knew Carrizo Springs would never be the same.

Chapter 4

A dry wind blew from the west as he was limping slowly up the street, a wind carrying the smell of death. The lone pistol shot he fired to end the sorrel horse's misery startled everyone. People were watching him, and he felt oddly uncomfortable under their stares, wondering if some would blame him for the deaths of loved ones and the stolen money. In his heart he knew he had done everything he could to stop the robbery. He'd put his life on the line the same as those who had died. Perhaps it had only been the luck of the draw that kept him alive today.

He came to the market where Arturo's wife and a small group of friends were gathered around the body. Anna Bustamante looked up when he arrived, mopping tears from her cheeks with a handkerchief.

"I'm sorry about Arturo," he said quietly. "That was a brave thing he did."

Anna nodded, sniffling back more tears. "I tried to stop him," she remembered in a strangled voice. "He would not listen to me . . ."

There was nothing more to be said, and he started to turn away, when an anguished cry came from the street corner where Cotter Evans lay. A neighbor was trying to comfort Alice Evans. Crow closed his eyes when he saw the pool of blood around the blacksmith's head. "Somebody oughta cover that body," he said, a remark no one else heard due to the woman's loud wails.

Sara Davis was sitting up on the boardwalk when he reached the front of the store. Rosa was tying a strip of cloth torn from the hem of her skirt around the wound to Sara's shoulder. Sara's eyes had a glazed-over look. She stared down at her husband. Swarms of hungry flies covered the body and the blood-soaked ground below the hitchrail.

"Why don't you take her inside," Crow said when Rosa noticed his presence. He said it gently.

Rosa understood. She touched Sara's cheek. "Come," she whispered. "There is nothing you can do here, señora."

As Rosa was helping Sara to her feet, Crow noticed a gathering farther to the south. A small group of people stood around another body at the edge of town. One of the bandits' horses was tied to the fence of Pedro Garza's goat pen.

Crow's strength was almost gone by the time he reached the group, and he was out of breath. He was immediately relieved when he discovered who was lying there. A dust-cloaked bandit was sprawled on his back with a bullet hole in his belly, leaking blood into a wagon rut beneath him. Pedro Garza smiled thinly when Crow walked up; he pointed to the saddled horse tethered to the fence.

"Some of the money did not leave Carrizo," Pedro said, "and this *bandido* is still alive."

A money sack dangled from the bandit's saddle horn.

Crow looked down at the wounded man. He saw a bearded face twisted in pain. Coal black eyes stared back at him. When the bandit noticed the badge pinned to the front of Crow's shirt, his lips parted in a snarl.

"Bastardo," he hissed, clenching discolored teeth. The look in his eyes was pure hatred.

Pedro spoke before Crow could think of anything to say.

"We should kill him," Pedro growled. "This is the one who shoot down my *amigo* Arturo!"

"He'll be dead pretty soon anyway," Crow insisted. "He's gut shot. No way to stop the bleeding inside him."

Pedro was not satisfied. "I say we kill him. It is what he deserves. Think of poor Anna and the little *niños* who will be orphans now."

"Killing him won't change anything," Crow said, noticing for the first time that Pedro held the bandit's pistol beside his leg. "Hand me that gun, Pedro. Then fetch me that bag of money so I can lock it up. I'd walk over there myself, only my leg's killin' me just now."

With some reluctance Pedro gave Crow the pistol. Some of the others standing around the bandit gave each other disapproving looks. Carlos Reyes, a cousin to Pedro, pointed to the wounded man.

"I say we should shoot him, Señor Crow," Carlos argued with heat in his voice.

Crow stuck the gun in his waistband as Pedro walked away to get the money. "He's as good as dead now," Crow said, with an eye on the bandit's belly wound. "He'll die slow this way and maybe it serves him right. There's another one down at the bank who ain't dead yet. I'm of the opinion there's been enough killing here today . . ."

Carlos gave the bandit a sneer; then he wheeled away and stalked off toward his adobe with his hands shoved in his pants pockets. One at a time, the other friends and relatives of Pedro Garza left the bandit to die. Pedro returned with the money bag and handed it to Crow; then he looked down at the dying man's face.

"Malo hombre," he said, turning his gaze down Main Street. "So many are dead because of Zambrano!"

Crow remembered the bandit leader and the load of buckshot fired at the front door of his office. "I reckon the big man was Luis Zambrano . . . the one riding the black horse. I had him in my gun sights twice and missed him both times. He's the one who blew off Harvey's head down at the bank. Wasn't any sense to it. Harvey was pleading with him . . ."

Pedro nodded once. "So many are dead now," he said again, the anger missing from his voice when his gaze passed over the scattered bodies a second time.

Crow glanced down at the money sack. "This town won't ever be like it was, that's for sure," he told Pedro quietly. "Leastways it'll be a hell of a long time before folks forget about what happened here today."

He saw Tinker walk out of the bank with Harriet Sims holding on to his arm. The old woman was a bit unsteady on her feet. When she saw Harvey Bascome's remains lying near the front door, she quickly turned her head and covered her eyes. Tinker put his arm around her waist and helped her past the headless corpse as rapidly as he could.

Looking south, a dust cloud grew smaller along the horizon. By his own quick count seven bandits had gotten away, taking most of the money with them. Although a few brave townspeople had cut the gang's number in half, it was little consolation. Four of the town's leading citizens were dead. Watching the dust move farther away, Crow was sure the bandits would never be punished for the raid. In a few hours they would be safe across the border and that would be the end of it. Thinking about it, he was suddenly boiling mad.

"The bastards oughta be made to pay," he growled, hobbling toward his office with the money bag. After he drank a few shots of tequila to calm his nerves, he meant to put the money back in the vault, but not before making sure Harriet was well enough to operate the safe combination.

He made the porch steps to his office with some difficulty and trudged inside, briefly taking note of the bullet scars across the front of the building, and the shattered front window. When the money was safely hidden at the bottom of a desk drawer, he took a bottle from a shelf above his desk and pulled the cork with his teeth. The first swallow of tequila burned down his throat. He sat down in his chair and let out a deep sigh, paying only passing notice to the pieces of glass over the desk top where the lantern globe had broken. Feeling drained, he drank again and rested, awaiting the soft glow from the tequila with the hope it might help ease the pain in his leg.

His gaze wandered to the glassless window. He took another drink, remembering the deadly gun battle. Somehow, he'd made it through the fight without losing his life.

It was an absurd idea, when a little while later he thought about the chances an armed posse might have of riding across the Rio Grande to get the town's money back. It would not be a lawful posse, for they would have no legal authority in Mexico. But with enough well-armed men who knew the region, he wondered if they would stand a chance of tracking down Zambrano, even if it took weeks to find him and root him out of his lair.

"It's a fool notion," he told himself, hearing a change in the way Alice Evans was crying outside. Through the open doorway he saw two men lift the blacksmith's body to carry it away.

The idea lingered, that he and a few good men might get the stolen money back. Remembering the money in his desk, he opened the drawer to peer into the bag. There was a sizable amount of currency, more than enough to offer a reward. Perhaps he could hire a paid gun or two down in Laredo to go with him, experienced men who knew the territory below the border. Laredo was a haven for gunslicks and bounty hunters. If he could find the right men for the job. . . .

Still, there were terrible risks. Zambrano was sure to have more men in his revolutionary band. Even if they found him, the odds would be in Zambrano's favor. On his own turf he would be twice as dangerous, knowing the lay of the land.

"It's a dumb idea," he said aloud, trying to envision what a full-fledged war with Zambrano's gang would be like. More lives would surely be lost. Was the stolen money worth it? Local ranchers and businessmen needed their money to survive. But would the price come too high in spilled blood?

Sipping more tequila, it rankled him that the bank robbers would go free. Mexican authorities might offer a token gesture, a promise to look into the matter, a promise that would never be kept. Unless someone from Carrizo Springs went after the money, it was sure to remain in Mexico forever.

"Two or three hired guns might do the trick," he said. Considering the possibilities, his mind drifted. He and Tinker could lead the expedition. If a few others from town and surrounding cattle ranches joined them, hand-picked men who could handle themselves, the plan had a chance of working. A slim chance, maybe.

The longer he thought about it, the more appeal he found in the notion that a few well-armed, determined men might stand a reasonable chance of getting the bank's money back. Pressing Zambrano from the rear, he might turn and fight to protect his booty before he could join up with more revolutionaries.

Then Crow remembered his injured leg. Sitting a saddle all day would keep his wound from healing. The gash needed stitches. The closest doctor was in Eagle Pass, but if he rode to Laredo with a twofold purpose, hiring experienced bounty hunters while seeing to his leg, perhaps they could cut Zambrano's trail by heading southwest below the border.

He pondered it further, examining every angle. Some of the townspeople would call his plan crazy. Others would refuse to go along out of fear. But if enough good men could be rounded up, it might work. Finding the right paid guns who would work for the chance to earn a reward offered the best hope of success for the venture. Experienced gunmen might turn the tide if the posse found Zambrano. Money would be the only way to secure the kind of fighting men the posse needed.

Crow remembered the sheriff at Laredo, a hard-bitten lawman by the name of Clint Sikes. Sikes would know where to find the hired gunmen he required. Sikes would probably laugh at the idea, that a posse without any legal authority could enter Mexico to retrieve the stolen bank

loot, going up against a revolutionary army led by Luis
Zambrano.

Crow gazed out the shattered remnants of his front
window. Worse than the danger of riding after the bandits
was the notion that nothing would be done about the
robbery and the killings in Carrizo Springs unless he
took some sort of action. The incident would be ignored
by Mexican authorities, and soon it would be forgotten
entirely. The deaths of four good citizens would go un-
punished. Without money, most of the ranchers and businessmen in Dimmit County would not be able to make
the winter.

"Somebody has to go after the sons of bitches," he
muttered, slowly bringing the bottle to his lips.

The sound of boots approaching the office ended his
thoughts on the subject momentarily. Tinker came up the
steps to peer around the door frame. Crow noticed that
the boy's face was still a waxy white.

"You okay, Jim Ed?" Tinker asked, glancing down at
Crow's bandage.

He nodded. "Hardly more'n a flesh wound, but it hurts
like hell and it's worse when I try to walk. I need to ask
you to attend to some unfinished business for me. Two of
the bandits are still alive . . . the feller you shot down at
the bank, and the one in front of Pedro's hut. See to it that
they both get taken someplace so's they can die without
making a public spectacle out of it. Things are bad
enough the way they are, what with four of our own
headed out to the graveyard. Ask a couple of men to help
you drag the rest of the bodies behind the office. Best to
get it done before they start to stink. You'll have to move
Harvey's body, too, seein' as he ain't got a family to see

to it and Harriet sure as hell ain't in no shape to make the arrangements for him."

Tinker swallowed. "I ain't lookin' forward to that chore, Jim Ed. Worst mess I ever saw, what they done to Harvey. I reckon I can try to do it with my eyes closed."

"I'll agree it isn't a very pretty sight," Crow said.

The deputy made a turn to leave the porch.

"Hold on a minute," Crow requested, feeling a bit sorry for the boy right then. "You did a hell of a job a while ago. It took a lot of courage to fight 'em the way you did. Just wanted you to know you handled the job real well."

"I was scared the whole time," Tinker replied sheepishly, looking down at his boots. "I don't figure it was courage that made me empty my gun. Truth is, I was just plain scared."

Crow understood. "A man would have to be completely crazy not to be afraid of a gun battle like that, son. It's natural to have some fear. You did yourself proud, and I wanted you to know I was grateful for the help."

Tinker glanced over his shoulder. "Wish we coulda stopped them before they got the money."

"We might still be able to do something about it if we could round up a few good men . . ."

At that, Tinker frowned. "Those owlhoots will be across the river before we could get up a posse, Jim Ed. I can't see how we could catch up to 'em in time."

"We wouldn't," Crow admitted, talking softly with his eyes to the street. "We'd have to cross the border to get that money back."

"Wouldn't be legal," Tinker replied, watching Crow's face.

After a pause, Crow said, "It's the only way. It would damn sure be risky, but it might work if we had a few good men . . ."

Chapter 5

Solemn faces watched him in the soft lantern glow. The hurriedly called assembly of men willing to form a posse had not produced the types he wanted. Tinker had ridden to most of the nearby ranches, returning just after dark to report that there were no volunteers among the cowboys earning day wages. Most range cowboys knew little about guns. Thus Crow regarded the small handful of local citizens gathered around him with sinking expectations for the success of his expedition. Goat herders knew even less about guns than the average cowpuncher.

He eyed Pedro Garza and Carlos Reyes. Both men were willing to go after Zambrano, but were they able to hold their own in an all-out gunfight? It didn't seem likely, and neither did he want any more dead men on his conscience.

"I'm planning to lead this posse across the river into Mexico," he continued, explaining the purpose for this meeting in front of the market. "Anyone who agrees to ride along is liable to be gone for a spell. And it'll be plenty dangerous if we find Zambrano's hideout. With what's left of the bank's money, I aim to offer a reward to whoever agrees to help us. It's my idea to hire a couple of professional bounty hunters down in Laredo if the right men can be found. I know the sheriff down there, and he'll know the kind of men I'm looking for."

"I will go," Pedro said. "I have a good rifle. Isabela will look after my goats while I am gone."

Crow decided against it almost at once. "You have little children, Pedro. Occurs to me we've got enough orphans to take care of, after what happened here today. I'm grateful for the offer . . . nobody can ever say you're short on courage, but I think it's best if you stay. That goes for the rest of you, too, I reckon. Me and Tinker will head down to Laredo to see if we can hire some paid guns. Thinking about it just now, that's about the only thing that makes any sense."

Pedro was still willing to go along. "I am not afraid," he said, "and I know how to shoot a gun."

Crow wagged his head. "I'll feel better if you stay." He turned to Tinker as others in the group started to leave the circle of lantern light. "Go saddle Dixie for me. Pack a change of clothes and some camping gear and I'll do the same. I expect we'll be gone a spell. Ask Alfredo to see to the bodies behind the office. Tell him I'll pay him something to dig the graves."

Tinker cast a look in the direction of the cantina. "If you ain't got no objections, Jim Ed, I'd like to say goodbye to Carmela before we go."

He gave the boy a sympathetic grin. "Got no objections," he said, taking a painful step away from the porch which made him wince. "Ask Alfredo to send along a couple of bottles of tequila. This damn leg is gonna hurt like hell for a day or two. If we ride most of the night we can make Laredo before daybreak. Don't take too long saying your goodbyes to that girl."

On his way across the road his limp worsened. His wound continued to swell. The gathering broke up when someone took down the lantern, and before Crow reached the office steps, the street was dark. He looked up at the stars as he climbed to the porch, wondering if his plan to go after the bank robbers was total madness. All afternoon he'd been thinking about it, judging their chances, weighing the odds. He concluded without much debate that he couldn't live with himself if he chose to do nothing at all about the raid. There were times when a man had to stand up and be counted for the things he believed in. Right or wrong, he knew he could not stomach ignoring what had happened. A man had to live with his conscience. He had to try something. . . .

"Sure was hard, sayin' *adios* to Carmela," Tinker remembered, guiding his horse down the starlit wagon road alongside Crow's big gray gelding.

"I reckon it's the same as leavin' a wife behind," Crow said. "Lately, you've taken a real fancy to that gal."

Tinker looked up at the night sky. "How come you never took yourself a wife, Jim Ed?"

The question made Crow chuckle, despite the throbbing in his injured thigh. "Never found a woman who could tolerate my peculiar ways, I suppose. I've been a bachelor so long that I reckon I'm set for life. I had a sweetheart once, back before the war. She quit writing after I'd been gone a year. Married a farmer with just one leg whilst I was off to war. She had two kids by the time I got home. She'd gotten fat as a town dog, and I was real glad I hadn't married her when I saw how wide she was. Women have a tendency to get fat after they get a man hitched. Remember that if you start thinking about marrying that little Mexican girl."

"Hadn't planned on gettin' hitched," Tinker replied quickly. "Besides, I wouldn't want folks to laugh at me if I was to up an' marry a woman like Carmela, on account of the way she earns her living. She ain't exactly the marryin' kind, if you get my drift."

Crow reached down to touch the bandage around his leg, checking for blood. The rag felt damp, and he knew he was bleeding again. "As far as I'm concerned there's no such thing as a marrying kind of woman."

For a time they listened to the click of horseshoes striking loose stones lying in the wagon ruts. Tinker appeared to be preoccupied, staring off at the dark brushland. Hardly a word had been said about the dangers they would face crossing the river to pursue the bandits.

"We could get shot full of holes down in Mexico, Jim Ed," Tinker said, an edge creeping into his voice.

Crow thought about the money in his saddlebags. "We won't chance it unless we can hire the right men to back us up. Just the two of us wouldn't amount to much going up against a bunch of revolutionaries. No way to tell how many men Zambrano has down there. We'll play it by ear, I reckon. If the odds are too long, we can turn tail and head back for the border."

Tinker looked over at Crow, studying his face. "How come you're doin' this?" he asked, frowning a little. "Nobody in town has a right to expect to get their money back after a robbery like the one we had. Everybody oughta know we done the best we could to prevent it."

"I suppose I've been wondering the same thing myself.

I guess you could call it pride. That money was my responsibility, in a manner of speaking. I've been taking the sheriff's pay for nigh unto twelve years, and if the truth was told, I never had to do all that much to earn it. Now something like this happens and it sticks in my craw like sand. If there's a way, I aim to get the money back. I'll sleep better at night, knowing I tried everything I could."

Tinker swallowed hard. "I sure hope both of us don't wind up sleepin' permanent because of it."

Crow turned in the saddle when he heard fear in Tinker's voice. "You've got a choice, son. It's not a requirement that you go with me. I won't think any less of you if you decide to pull stakes. Going to Mexico ain't a part of the deputy's job."

"My mind's done made up to go, Jim Ed. But every now and then, when I get to thinkin' about what might happen, my belly does a flip flop. I ain't all that brave to start with, and when those bullets started flyin' this afternoon, I never was so scared in all my life. My hands was shakin' so bad I could hardly hang on to my rifle. It was pure luck when I shot that Mexican in front of the bank. Fact is, I was shakin' so bad I was lucky to hit anything."

"Maybe you're being too hard on yourself, Tinker. I'd say you did yourself real proud today. It took guts to keep throwing lead at that bunch, outnumbered like we were."

Tinker allowed a silence to pass. "How's the leg?" he asked a moment later, as they were crossing a gentle rise where the road twisted southeast.

"It hurts some. If you'll pass me one of those bottles of agave juice, maybe it'll help."

Tinker removed a bottle from his saddlebags. Crow pulled the cork and took a generous swallow, then another. Off in the distance a coyote howled and the sound made him shiver. Right then, that coyote call was about the lonesomest sound in the world.

The city sheriff's office sat near the end of the road at the river crossing into Mexico. Morning sunlight gave the clapboard building an unnatural orange glow. Laredo was still asleep at this early hour, and the city streets were empty. Crow eased his weight from the saddle, testing his sore leg when he reached the ground. Dried blood had turned the bandage an angry red. He limped to the porch rail and tied off his gray, sighting the tiny beacon of a lantern globe shinning behind the office window.

"Let's hope Clint has coffee made," he said, climbing to the porch with the aid of a porch post.

When he opened the door, he found a familiar face near the potbelly stove, a face hardened by wind and sun and the risks of a dangerous job. A drooping handlebar mustache flecked with gray lifted as Crow entered the room, revealing thin lips parting in a smile when the sheriff saw him.

"I'll be damned if it ain't Jim Ed Crow. Appears you got that leg caught in a bear trap someplace."

Crow hobbled across the room to shake hands. "Howdy, Clint. It's been a spell." He aimed a thumb over his shoulder. "Meet my deputy, Tinker Warren. You're wrong about the bear hunting, ol' hoss. A bear would starve to death around Carrizo Springs this year. Been dry as popcorn lately. But it's been a good year for Mexican bandits, and that's the reason we're here. If you'll part with some of that coffee on the stove, I'll tell you about it."

Clint dropped Crow's hand to take Tinker's briefly, the

smile leaving his face. "Help yourself to the coffee. Tell me this yarn about *bandidos*. When did they hit you?"

Crow took a clean tin cup from a peg above the stove and handed another to Tinker. "We had a visit from Luis Zambrano's bunch yesterday afternoon. Fourteen of them, to be exact. They robbed our bank and killed four good men. I got this scrape on my leg during the fracas and felt damn lucky to be alive when the shooting was over. They hightailed it for the river soon as it was over, which I'm sure don't surprise you none. We managed to get seven of 'em before they rode out. I suppose I'll notify the Texas Rangers while I'm here . . . we still don't have a telegraph line through Carrizo. The country's too damn hard to dig the holes for the poles, I reckon."

The sheriff was frowning. "Tell me why the hell you rode all night to get here, Jim Ed? Eagle Pass is a hell of a lot closer, and you know it as well as me."

Crow poured coffee and settled into a vacant chair against the office wall before he answered. "I came down here to hire some paid guns. Me and my deputy are going after the money, if we can find the right men to side with us."

Clint cocked his head sideways, like he hadn't heard quite right. "Have you gone completely loco?" he asked, trying to read Crow's expression.

"Maybe," Crow replied, sipping from the cup gingerly to keep from burning his lips and tongue. "I can't just turn my back on it, Clint. Every rancher and businessman in town is flat busted now without their saved money. Carrizo is liable to dry up and blow away unless we can get that loot back."

"What makes you think you can get it back?" the sheriff asked, without making any effort to hide his low opinion of the idea. "Word is, Zambrano has raised himself an army. The fourteen men who paid you a call likely weren't no more than a handpicked few of the ones he trusted. Hellfire, Jim Ed, you've lived along the border long enough to know you can't just wander off down there totin' a gun. That badge you're wearin' don't mean spit below the Rio Grande. If Comandante Obregon hears that you crossed over to go after stolen money, he's liable to toss you in a Mexican jail and throw away the key."

Crow shrugged. "I'd sorta figured he'd be willing to help us. The *federales* ought to be just as interested in putting a stop to Zambrano's activities as we are, seems to me."

"You're forgetting about the money," Clint replied knowingly. "If Obregon finds it, he'll keep it for himself, and you'll have risked your hide for nothing. Most of the *federales* I'm acquainted with are crooked. They won't let you ride back across the river with it, and they're sure as hell liable to throw you in jail if they find out what you're doin' down there."

A shooting pain down Crow's leg made him grimace. Before any more was said, Clint motioned to the door.

"I'll go fetch Doc Grimes so he can take a look at you, an' while I'm gone you'd best do some hard thinkin' about that empty-headed notion. Until this mornin', I'd have sworn you had good sense, Jim Ed. But you've got me to wondering now."

The sheriff walked out of the office. Somewhere in an alley behind the building a donkey brayed. As soon as the sound of Clint's boots faded, Tinker turned to Crow with a worried look on his face.

"Have you been listenin' to what that sheriff said?" he asked.

Crow nodded thoughtfully, staring at the far wall where rows of Wanted circulars hung above the sheriff's desk. "I heard every word he said. I never claimed this would be easy, and I told you once before you can pull out any time you take the fancy to it. Everything depends on being able to hire the right gunmen for this kind of job. Without them it won't work."

Tinker leaned against the door frame, swirling grounds at the bottom of his cup. "I said I was stayin', Jim Ed. If you decide to go, I'll be right there beside you. That don't mean I won't be a touch worried about it. I ain't had hardly any experience with this sort of thing."

A voice from the back room containing the jail cells interrupted their conversation. Until now, Crow had not noticed the door was ajar or known anyone was listening to them.

"Hey you out front! There's two of us back here with guns for hire!"

Crow smiled and shook his head. "Can't hardly see how you'd be any use to me," he replied, giving Tinker a wink. "What good are a couple of jailbirds locked up in an iron cage?"

"You could talk that bigmouth lawman into lettin' us out," the man replied gruffly. "Me an' Bill have tracked desperados all over the territories, and we know how to shoot. Ask Bill if you doubt my word."

"Shut up, Roy," another voice snapped, sounding muffled.

Simple curiosity got the best of Crow. He climbed out of his chair and hobbled to the doorway. When he opened the door he saw a man standing in a poorly lit cell with huge, hamlike hands clamped to the bars. A whisker-stubbled face was staring back at him. On a cot against the far wall of the cell another man lay with his head propped on a folded blanket. Crow examined the pair for a moment as his eyes adjusted to the bad light.

"Who are you?" he asked, not really caring just then, only passing time until Clint got back with the doctor.

The man at the bars said, "I'm Roy Hyde and this here's my partner, Bill Middleton. We overheard what you were sayin' to the sheriff, and we're damn sure the gents you need if you want good shootists fer the ride down to Mexico. Sheriff Sikes jailed us over a fight we had with a saloonful of Mexicans. Me an' Bill damn sure didn't back down when those greasers called us out. If the sheriff hadn't come along when he did, we'd have killed every one of the sorry sons of bitches."

Crow examined Roy Hyde briefly in slanted sunlight from a barred window of the cell, until his attention was drawn to the figure lying on the bunk. Bill Middleton was watching him with a pair of the coldest gray eyes Crow had ever seen.

"We can't use jailbirds," he said, sounding tired, although in the back of his mind Crow found himself wondering.

Chapter 6

The stitches across his thigh helped some when he and Tinker joined Clint Sikes for a late breakfast at an eatery across the road from the jail. They took chairs before the sheriff spoke.

"You'll be makin' a big mistake if you go, Jim Ed."

A waitress brought them coffee in china cups.

"Maybe," Crow replied thoughtfully, staring blankly out a cafe window at the street. Wagons and donkey carts rattled past laden with all manner of goods, though he paid little notice to what was being transported through Laredo. "Hard to explain why I've made up my mind to try it. The folks around Carrizo depended on me, I suppose, and I let them down. If there's a way to get some of that money back, I aim to see if I can pull it off. Nearly everybody in Dimmit County is flat broke now, and some will go out of business without their savings."

"You could go out of business yourself," Clint remarked dryly. "A bullet ends a lawman's career in a hell of a hurry. It weren't your fault when that bunch robbed your bank and got away clean. You told me you did everything you could to stop them."

"There was just the two of us," Crow remembered. "We poured all the lead we could into the street; but there were just too damn many of them, and they had us pinned down. A few storekeepers tried to lend us a hand and got themselves killed for their trouble. Worst tight spot I ever was in, Clint. Bullets flyin' every which way. It was as bad as anything I saw in the war."

The sheriff made a face. "You could be headed into a bigger mess below that river. No tellin' how many soldiers Zambrano has raised by now. When word gets out that he's got money to hire more mercenaries, it'll only get worse. If you're fool enough to go, you'll be ridin' into a hornet's nest. The way I see it, you've got no obligation to the citizens of Carrizo Springs to do any more than you already did. You did your best to protect their money, and that's damn sure all they can expect."

Right then, Crow wished for another topic of conversation. It was evident Clint didn't think much of the plan. "I could use some advice when it comes to hiring a few men to ride with us," he continued. "A few names, maybe. Some men I could trust."

At that, the sheriff shook his head. "There ain't no such thing as hired guns who can be trusted. Seems like you'd know that already. The ones hangin' around local saloons are on the lookout for easy pickings. Soon as the going got rough they'd hightail it for safer surrounds."

Crow found himself thinking about the pair in the Laredo jail. "What's the story on the two prisoners you've got?"

Clint's eyelids narrowed as he examined Crow's face. "I wouldn't trust either one of them and neither should you. They hail from up in Kansas . . . a couple of bounty hunters. They've been hangin' around town for a month or two, claiming to be on the lookout for a wanted feller by the name of Cody Wade who was headed for the border. When they first rode in I wired the U.S. marshal up in Abilene about 'em, figuring they were up to no good down here. I'll show you the telegram I got back. Bill Middleton, the one with the funny-colored eyes, is a back shooter, a dangerous bastard if ever there was one. That wire suggested I run them both out of town if I wanted any peace and quiet. Roy Hyde is a mean son of a bitch . . . figures he's tougher than any man wearing boot leather. If you ask me, I'd say he's plumb loco. Those two are nothin' but trouble, Jim Ed. I'd look elsewhere if you're dead set on going after the money."

"I need hard men," Crow argued. "It won't be any church social, tangling with Zambrano."

"You'd be committin' suicide with Middleton and Hyde behind your back. If you got your hands on the money somehow, that pair would kill you for it the first time your back was turned."

Tinker toyed with his coffee cup. "Maybe we oughta listen to the sheriff, Jim Ed. I ain't exactly lookin' to get killed and neither are you. Takin' that pair of rattlesnakes with us don't hardly make any sense, according to my way of thinkin'."

Crow arched an eyebrow when he looked across the table. "You got any better notions on how we get the loot back?"

The deputy's cheeks colored a little. "Maybe it can't be done," he replied, avoiding Crow's stare.

"The boy's makin' sense," Clint said flatly. "I'd think it over real hard before I put my neck in a noose for sacks of money that wasn't mine in the first place. Folks around Carrizo Springs will understand."

"Most of them are my friends," Crow said quietly. "They depended on me and I let them down. I couldn't face them unless I knew I'd tried everything. Some of them can't make the winter without hard cash. I reckon I told you that already."

The sheriff's face mirrored his frustration with Crow's refusal to listen to reason. "You know that border country as well as me," he said, sighing. "Roughest land on earth when it comes to horses and men. If the land don't get you first, you'll be lookin' for a fight with one of the meanest sons of bitches ever to come out of Mexico. Ask anybody who knows Zambrano, an' they'll tell you he's hard as nails, a cold-blooded killer. On top of that, you're aimin' to hire a crew of back shooters and murderers to back your play when you get there. We've known each other a long time, Jim Ed, and I always had you figured for a man with good sense. Only what you're aimin' to do now don't make any sense at all."

Crow aimed his face down at the tabletop. "Hearin' you say it makes it sound crazy. If you've got a better idea, I'll listen to it."

"Go back home," Clint said. "Explain to everybody that there wasn't anything else you could do. File a report with the Texas Rangers and leave it at that. You're just one man and you've got no legal authority across the river. It's out of your hands now."

"I couldn't face my friends," Crow protested, knowing he was wasting his breath with Clint. "I've got to try to do something so my conscience will leave me alone."

The sheriff's expression softened some. "Your conscience is gonna get you killed, old friend, if you cross the Rio Grande to look for Zambrano. When you come to your senses, you'll see I'm right. You an' the boy here oughta rest up a day or two and then ride back to Carrizo Springs . . . when the soreness works itself out of that leg. The way things are now, at least the two of you are still alive."

The waitress returned with more coffee. Crow thought about what Clint said as they ordered ham and eggs for breakfast. In his heart, he knew he wasn't going back to Carrizo without making some sort of attempt to get the money back. "I'd like to talk to those two jailbirds," he said later, after the waitress left. "If you've got no objections."

Muscles hardened in the sheriff's cheeks briefly; then he nodded. "I reckon it won't hurt for you to talk to 'em. But you remember what I said about how dangerous they are. And I want to show you that wire from the sheriff up in Abilene. They're nothin' but trouble on the hoof, that pair."

Bill Middleton eyed Crow with suspicion. Roy Hyde wore a flat, disinterested expression while he listened to the story of the bank robbery. Midday heat trapped inside the jail cell had grown stifling, worsening the faint smells of urine and unwashed bodies. Beyond the cell window sounds from the city—the creak of axles, the rattle of harness chains and the shuffle of shod hooves on powder-dry caliche roads—filled the brief silences when Crow paused to recall a minor detail.

Middleton's pale eyes narrowed. "How many men does this Zambrano have with him now?"

Crow shrugged. "No way to know for sure. He rode into Carrizo Springs with fourteen bandits, and we were able to cut that number in half. They killed four local citizens during the robbery."

"Appears you caught one in the leg," Hyde said, merely glancing at Crow's bandaged thigh.

"My deputy and me were lucky to get out with our skins."

Middleton seemed pensive. "How much does the job pay?"

"I hadn't decided that yet. I wanted to know if you two were interested first."

"Could be we are," Middleton replied carefully. "Kinda depends on the money. And the size of that army we'd be up against."

Hyde rubbed his chin with thick, calloused fingers. "You'd have to get us out of here first, Sheriff. That saloonkeeper has brung charges against us for the damage we did. He claims we tore up better'n a hundred dollars' worth of his furniture."

"That can be arranged," Crow said, "if we strike a bargain."

"You still ain't said how much it pays," Middleton reminded.

Crow leaned back against the bars of the cell. "The way I see it, there's two things you get paid for. First there's the pay to ride down there to look things over. If the risks are too high, we ride back emptyhanded and that'll be the end of it. If it looks like we can pull the job, there'll be a reward for helping us get the money back to Laredo."

"You make it sound mighty easy," Hyde said, glancing at his partner. "If we run into a couple hundred Mexicans, earnin' that reward is gonna be nigh unto impossible."

"It's a chance you'll have to take," Crow answered. "I said I'd pay you for riding down to look it over. Even that may take a spell. Finding Zambrano won't be all that easy. We could be down there a couple of weeks, maybe."

"How much," Middleton demanded. "Let's stop all this pussyfootin' around and talk money."

Crow took a deep breath. He would be spending money that was not his to hire the gunmen. Another thing had begun to bother him now. During the course of the brief conversation, he discovered he was developing a strong dislike for both men, and just the idea of giving them money didn't sit well. "I'd pay five hundred dollars to each of you for helping us find Zambrano. Half up front, the other half when we get back. Sheriff Sikes will hold the money. You can claim it even if we look things over and decide the odds are too long against us. The five hundred will be yours, either way."

"What about the reward?" Middleton asked, leaning forward on the edge of his bunk. "How much is that gonna be, if we get the money back?"

Crow knew the amount had to be enough to interest the two bounty hunters, enough to make them take big risks. "I figure a thousand more apiece is real generous. It can be the biggest pay day you ever had."

A lopsided grin widened Roy Hyde's mouth. "You got my attention just then," he said. "For a thousand dollars each me an' Bill can kill a whole bunch of Mexicans."

"There's a hitch, ain't there?" Middleton asked, never taking his eyes from Crow, speaking in a voice like dry sand.

Crow shook his head. "The only hitch is that there's no reward unless we get the bank's money back. Killing Mexicans won't be enough to earn it. When the money crosses the Rio Grande tied to my saddle horn, you get paid a thousand in cash, plus the other half of the five hundred I promised you."

"Makes it fifteen hundred," Hyde said.

Suspicion still showed in Middleton's eyes. "How many of us will there be?" he asked quickly.

"Maybe only the four of us," Crow replied. "I'd hire one or two more if I could find the right men."

"That don't hardly sound like enough to take on a whole goddamn Mexican army," Middleton remarked.

"We won't be looking for a direct confrontation. We'll avoid a head-on fight if we can. All we're after is the money."

Middleton scowled. "This Zambrano, he won't be stupid. He'll have himself surrounded by bodyguards, protecting him and his loot. Besides that, down there in Mexico a white man will stick out like a sore thumb. They'll see us coming for a country mile."

"I never said it would be easy," Crow replied.

Hyde was looking at Tinker now, wearing a disgusted look. "Your deputy ain't nothin' but a kid. I'd bet the price of a new hat he won't amount to much in a gunfight. The way I figure it, that only leaves three of us to do the real fightin'."

"You're wrong about him," Crow said evenly. "Don't let his age fool you. He can shoot straight, and he's plenty long on courage."

Tinker said nothing, looking askance, although Crow was sure the remark from Hyde stung him a little.

Middleton stirred. He got up from his bunk and sauntered over to the cell window. Crow examined the Kansan more carefully in the sunlight beaming through the bars. Middleton was a lanky, hard-twisted man of about thirty, he guessed. There was something about the bounty hunter that made Crow uneasy, something more than the warning from Clint Sikes about not turning his back on him. Some men had a way about them, in Crow's experience, an intangible thing that warned others away. Middleton was like that. Being near him made Crow more and more uncomfortable.

Roy Hyde, on the other hand, seemed more predictable. He was a hulking, bullish man, roughly the same age as his partner, who said what was on his mind. Crow had seen his kind during the war, the fearless types who charged headlong into a fight without considering the consequences.

"Me an' Roy'll talk it over," Middleton said a moment later, after appearing to deliberate Crow's proposition. He turned from the window and stared at Crow for a time. "Let's get one thing straight, Sheriff. If we decide to go down yonder with you, it'll be for the money, and the both of us aim to live long enough to spend it. When we get a look at the setup, then we'll decide if the fight can be won. Nobody else is gonna decide that for us. Make damn sure you understand that before you make us that offer again."

Crow nodded and pushed away from the bars to exit the cell door. "Fair enough," he said. "Think it over while we ask around town to see who else is available. We'll be back before it gets dark to hear your answer. If you take the job, we'll be leaving at first light tomorrow morning."

Middleton eyed his partner, then shook his head. "I reckon you can have our answer now. Me an' Roy'll go down there for the five hundred, but that's all we're agreein' to for now."

Crow locked the cell door behind him and walked into

the office with Tinker close at his heels. After hanging the key ring on a peg above the sheriff's desk, he led the way out on the tiny front porch where Clint Sikes rested on a bench in the shade to watch traffic moving up and down the street.

"I don't like that Middleton feller," Tinker said when they were out of earshot from the men inside. "Fact is, can't say as I care for either one of 'em much."

Crow hooked his thumbs in his gunbelt, idly watching the river crossing into Mexico where wagons and carts labored through the shallow water toward Nuevo Laredo. "I'll agree they aren't all that likable, but we don't aim to take up homesteading with them. I've got a feeling they're the right men for the job."

"I say you're dead wrong," Sikes said. "It won't surprise me none to hear that the two of you were killed in your bedrolls down there if you take Bill and Roy along."

Crow set his sights on a saloon named the Broken Spoke near the river crossing. For the time being he ignored the sheriff's remark, although by the look on Tinker's face, his deputy had been paying close attention to the warning. "Believe I'll wander down to that drinking parlor. If we could find one or two more gents who can use a gun . . ."

Sikes was frowning. "There's one more owlhoot you can talk to, seein' as it appears you're dead set on tryin' to get yourself killed. He's across the river now, because he's a wanted man in Texas. You could take those badges off before you ride over to this little cantina I know and ask for Lee Johnson . . ."

Chapter 7

Curtained windows of the low-roofed adobe building admitted very little sunlight. At first glance, the cantina seemed to be empty. Near the doorway, Crow hesitated, to allow his eyes to adjust to the darkness, catching the scent of tequila and stale smoke before he walked inside.

The faint red glow of a cigar tip alerted him to someone's presence at the back of the room. There, seated with his back to the wall, a dark figure watched Crow and Tinker from the darker shadow of a low-pulled hat brim. Crow stepped into the cantina, knowing he was outlined in the doorway by sunlight from the street, a chance he would have to take to inquire about Lee Johnson here. Tinker followed Crow across the hard-packed dirt floor to a makeshift bar fashioned from rough planking atop wooden kegs. A slender Mexican bartender watched them approach.

"*Sí*, señors," the barman said expectantly.

"A bottle of good tequila and some information. I'm looking for Lee Johnson."

The Mexican's eyes strayed briefly to the corner table, and Crow knew without being told the man with the cigar was Johnson. "I've got a business proposition for Johnson, if he's interested," Crow went on, digging in a pocket for some silver. "I was told he would be here, and that he'd be interested in making some money."

The barkeep placed a bottle in Crow's hand. *"Por favor,* señor. I do not know this man . . . Johnson. But if you wish, you may leave word for him here and I will see if someone can deliver your message."

"There isn't time for that," Crow replied. "We're leaving in the morning. I've got a job to do down here in Mexico, and I need a man who can handle himself."

A chair scraped softly in the corner. The cigar glowed a brighter red. "What sort of job you got?" a wary voice asked.

Crow turned. "A dangerous job, maybe. But the pay is good. There's liable to be some shooting. I was told Lee Johnson is a good hand with a gun."

"Where'd you get your information, mister?"

At that, Crow chuckled softly. "The Laredo sheriff. He told me where to look for him. Also said Johnson is wanted back in Texas for killing a man."

For a moment there was silence. Crow waited, examining the man holding the cigar, now that his eyes had grown accustomed to the bad light. The first thing he noticed about Lee Johnson came as a surprise; Johnson was a black man, a fact Clint Sikes failed to mention.

"Are you a bounty hunter lookin' to claim the reward out on me?" Johnson asked, admitting he was the man Crow sought as a Colt pistol appeared suddenly above the tabletop.

Crow wagged his head. "If you're Lee Johnson, I'm looking to hire you. You can put that gun away . . . you won't need it. I have a proposition for you, if you're interested."

"Maybe I am and maybe I ain't. You said this job could be dangerous. First off, you better explain jus' how dangerous the work can be. I'll own up to bein' Lee Johnson, but the gun stays in my hand 'til I know who you are, and what you're after. You can bring that jug over to the table and sit, if you've a mind to, while I hear 'bout this here proposition."

Crow fisted the tequila by the bottleneck and took two shot glasses before he ambled toward the table. In the pale light from a curtained window across the room, he could see more of the gunman's face. Pausing beside a chair, he put the bottle and glasses down. Johnson watched him carefully as he took a seat and waited for Tinker to do the same. After they both had chairs, Johnson relaxed his gun hand and then slowly placed the Colt .44 on the tabletop in front of him, within easy reach.

"I'm Jim Ed Crow," he began, "sheriff of Carrizo Springs. Don't let that worry you none. I'm here unofficially. This here's my deputy, Tinker Warren. We're headed into Mexico to look for a gang of bandits. They robbed our little bank yesterday and killed four people. I aim to try to get our money back if I can."

The broad, angular face below the flat-brim hat broke into a curious half smile, although Johnson's face still had a savage countenance, even when he grinned. His eyes remained fixed on Crow without a trace of friendliness. "You're talkin' like a crazy man," he said quietly, almost a whisper, hard to hear even in the silence of the empty cantina. He flicked ash from the end of his cigar and reached for the bottle, still watching Crow warily as he poured three glasses of tequila.

"Maybe I am a little crazy to think I can do it," Crow continued. "But that money belongs to my friends. Most of them will be wiped out without the cash they had saved."

"Bein' wiped out is better'n bein' dead," Johnson said as he lifted the shot glass to his lips. He knocked back his drink in one swallow. "I don't figger you know much about Mexico or you wouldn't have such a crazy notion. Things ain't the same here as over in Texas."

Crow sipped his own drink slowly. "I know the border country pretty well. For the most part there isn't any law down here. I plan to track those bandits if I can. Look things over if I find them and see if there's a way to get the money without getting killed. I'm hiring a few men to go along, men who know how to fight. I'll pay five hundred dollars, half up front, the rest when we get back, regardless. If we get the money, there's a thousand more to each man who helps me get it back across the Rio Grande."

The grin left Johnson's face almost at once. "That's a hell of a lot of money for soldiering pay, Sheriff. How many soldiers do you aim to hire at that price?"

"Three, if you go along. I've made the offer to a couple of bounty hunters locked up in the Laredo jail."

Johnson stiffened a little. "Me an' bounty hunters can't make no music together. There's a reward out on me over at Brenham. A couple of bounty hunters might try to claim it and haul my carcass back across the river."

"You've got my word I won't let that happen," Crow replied. "You'll be safe, so long as you work for me."

The gunman scowled. "You talk mighty tough, Sheriff. How do I know you can keep your word on somethin' like that?"

"It's simple arithmetic. The two bounty hunters can't earn the money I'm offering unless I come back alive to draw it out of the bank in Laredo. They'll do what I tell them to do, so they can get paid."

Johnson filled his glass again, puffing on the stump of his cigar, thoughtful now. "Somethin' about this still don't add up. I never met a lawman who'd set out to break the law, hirin' a couple of bounty hunters and a man wanted by the law to get some stolen money back. When I say it out loud like that, I can't make myself believe you're on the level, mister."

"It's a straight business proposition," Crow replied, "and I'm acting on my own down here, as a private citizen. I've got no authority. This is a simple business deal."

The gunman downed his second drink while trying to read Crow's expression. "Tell me a little more," he said. "Who are the two bounty hunters, and who's the bandit you're goin' after."

Crow decided to deliver the bad news first. "The bandit is Luis Zambrano."

Johnson's eyes widened perceptibly. He bit down on the cigar and talked around it. "Zambrano ain't some common holdup man and you oughta know it as well as me if you've lived around here very long. He's got himself a regular army down close to Hidalgo. Every *federale* in the north of Mexico is lookin' for him, so how the hell you figger you can find him?"

"I was told you used to be a scout for the army," Crow said, remembering the last thing Clint Sikes told him as he was leaving the money in his saddlebags with the sheriff for safekeeping. "I'd hoped you could pick up Zambrano's trail where he crossed the river yesterday. Sheriff

Sikes told me you scouted for Crook during the Indian wars."

The gunman refilled his glass. "I did a little scouting for the cavalry. I might be able to follow those tracks, but when we got to Zambrano's hideout we'd find ourselves in a fix. Word is, he's got a bunch of revolutionaries near Hidalgo. Five men won't have a snowball's chance in hell of getting close to him. We'd all wind up dead for our trouble. None of us would live to collect that money you're offerin'.''

"If it looks too tricky, we turn around and head back. I'd leave that choice up to you and the other two. Anybody who wants out can head for the border. I'll leave word with Sheriff Sikes to bring the other half of the five hundred to Nuevo Laredo soon as you get here with a note from me saying your pay is due. You wouldn't have to cross the river to get the rest of what I owe you."

Johnson leaned forward in his chair. "You're real serious about this, ain't you? You've got all the angles figgered out."

Crow sipped the last of his tequila, nodding once. "I intend to try it. The townspeople back in Carrizo Springs are depending on me. Without their savings, most of them are finished, and I won't have it on my conscience that I let Zambrano rob them without doing everything I could to get the money back for them."

"Sounds to me like you take the sheriffing job too serious. It can't pay all that much."

Crow shrugged. "It isn't the money. Those people are my friends."

Johnson picked up his Colt and dropped it back into a well-worn holster tied low on his right leg. He watched Crow thoughtfully for a moment. "You've got too many principles to suit me, Sheriff Crow. Plenty of men have died believin' in just causes and the principle of things. Me, I ain't built that way, but I'll go with you down to Hidalgo for five hundred dollars, half paid in advance like you said. I'll read what sign there is and take you wherever the tracks lead. But don't count on me throwing in with you after that. I like this ol' black skin without any extra holes in it."

"That's all I'm asking," Crow said, feeling the weight of a sleepless night in the saddle now. "You can make up your mind about the rest of it when we see how many men Zambrano has around him, where he's holed up, how tough it will be to get to the place where he stashed the money. Despite what you may think, I'm not looking for a way to get myself killed. If the job looks too difficult, we'll pull out. I can look my friends in the eye and tell them I did everything I could."

Something Crow said left the gunman mildly amused. "Can't say as I ever met a man who put so much stock in friendship," he said, grinning again.

Crow sighed, noticing that his eyelids felt heavy. "A lesson from the war, I suppose. There were times when all a man had was a friend to pull him through." He got up and motioned Tinker toward the door. "We'll pull out at sunup tomorrow. I have to go back to make the arrangements to get Middleton and Hyde out of jail before we get some shut-eye."

Johnson came up from his chair, his expression suddenly turned hard, his eyes becoming fiery pinpoints. "Would that be Bill Middleton?" he asked coldly, bunching powerful muscles across his thick shoulders as though he meant to spring across the table before Crow could back away.

"The same, I reckon," Crow answered guardedly, wondering about the gunman's strange reaction. "What makes you ask?"

A silence lingered. Tinker aimed an anxious look in Crow's direction, sensing the nearness of trouble. Johnson remained frozen, staring into Crow's eyes, wearing a look that could only be described as hatred.

"I know him," Johnson said, whispering again, finally relaxing the muscles in his heavy arms. "He got on my trail west of Brenham and followed me all the way to the border. We had a run-in close to Cuero at a little trading post. I came within a whisker of killing him, only he had a partner and I didn't like the odds. Me and him are liable to tangle if we ride together, Sheriff. Maybe it ain't such a good idea that I go with you."

"I need all the guns I can get," Crow said. "The two of them can't make a big pay day unless we're successful, so they'd be fools to do anything that might weaken our chances of getting the money back. I'll talk to Middleton . . . make sure he understands that I won't tolerate any trouble between the two of you."

For a moment Johnson seemed uncertain; then he raised a gnarled finger and aimed it across the table. "You warn him, Sheriff. Tell him I'll kill him this time if he makes a move agin' me."

Crow nodded. "We'll be here at first light. I'll buy plenty of ammunition in Laredo, just in case we get ourselves in a shootout. We can pack enough supplies for a couple of weeks, and some repeating rifles. I'll have the first half of your money, too, so be ready to ride at dawn."

The gunman relaxed. He shook his head. "I'll be saddled and ready. Mind you, tell Middleton and his partner what I said just now. I swear I'll kill 'em both if they make a play."

"I'll tell them," Crow said, swinging for the door. He walked out behind Tinker and mounted the gray.

As they were riding away from the cantina, Tinker looked over his shoulder. "That nigra is just askin' to get hisself killed by them bounty hunters, Jim Ed."

Crow thought about the three men they would be taking along. "I'm not quite so sure it won't be the other way around," he said as they made their way toward the river crossing, remembering Lee Johnson's catlike moves. "I wouldn't want to wager on the outcome. Johnson has natural quickness. I'd hate like hell to have to go up against him with a six-shooter, or a Bowie knife."

Tinker's face turned a lighter shade of pale. "We could get ourselves caught in a cross fire if they decide to try to kill each other. Maybe takin' all three of 'em ain't such a good idea."

He heard the concern in Tinker's voice. "It takes a certain breed to make a top gun hand, son. A man who kills for pay has to be hard—ruthless—he can't afford a conscience. I expect we'll have our hands full trying to keep them apart until we find those bandits, but I never figured we'd have the pick of the litter for this sort of job anyway. It boils down to the fact that we've got damn few choices. We take the toughest men we can find, and hope the men Luis Zambrano has with him aren't any tougher."

"Lordy," Tinker said quietly, as if he were talking to himself, "I ain't rightly sure I belong with this outfit now."

Crow looked over at his deputy with sympathy. "You can head back any time you take the notion. I wouldn't hold it against you."

"I'm stayin'," Tinker said, although now, his voice lacked conviction.

They spurred their horses down a narrow side street that would take them to the river. To the west and south lay endless miles of empty Mexican desert. Once, before they reached the crossing, Crow looked over his shoulder at the barren land, wondering if he and his young deputy would survive a journey across the inhospitable wastes. Thinking about it now, he felt the beginnings of fear. It wasn't the land he feared, for he knew it as well as most men. They would be in the company of three hardened killers, seeking a gang of ruthless cutthroats where the only law was the law of the gun. Any man with good sense was due to be afraid of such an undertaking.

Chapter 8

He stood before the bars to address the two Kansans after taking supper in the company of Clint Sikes. He'd made the arrangements for their release tomorrow morning and paid a small fine in their behalf. Sheriff Sikes hadn't liked Crow's plan any better at suppertime and still argued against it.

"I've bailed you out," Crow began. "My deputy is seeing to your horses. There's an added wrinkle, one you need to know about. Unless I have your word that there won't be any trouble, you'll be staying in this iron cage until your time is served."

"What's this new wrinkle?" Middleton asked cautiously. He sat up and swung his legs off the bunk, staring at Crow with mounting suspicion.

"It better not have anythin' to do with how much money we get," Hyde warned.

"The money's the same. We've added a man to the expedition, a man by the name of Lee Johnson."

The men looked at each other quickly. "What's that got to do with us?" Middleton asked, silencing his slower-witted partner before Hyde could speak. "Can't say as I've ever heard of no Lee Johnson before."

Crow rocked back on his boot heels. "I know differently. I spoke to Johnson this afternoon, and he told me about the run-in you had at Cuero. I'm warning you to leave Johnson alone while we're down in Mexico. If anything happens to him, neither one of you will get the rest of the money I promised you. The reward for his arrest is posted in the office, so add it up. Three hundred dollars is considerable shy of the pay you'll get from me when we get back, with or without the stolen bank loot."

Middleton jumped to his feet. "He's a damn nigra! He shot a white man down at Brenham. His kind deserves to be hung!"

It was Crow's turn to feel amusement. "All you care about is the reward posted for his capture, so save the speeches. I need men with his particular talents, so either I have your word that you'll leave him alone, or you stay in this jail until you've done your time. Remember what I said . . . if anything happens to Lee Johnson, neither one of you gets paid."

"That ain't fair!" Hyde protested angrily, glancing at his partner. "That darkie is a wanted man. You're a lawman, so it ain't right that you'd take his side!"

"I'm taking it," Crow replied evenly. "Nobody makes a move against Johnson while we're in Mexico. I want that understood."

Some of the tension flowed out of Middleton. He relaxed his balled fists and finally shrugged. "I still don't like it, that you'd take a shine to some nigra who killed a white man. But I reckon me an' Roy can tolerate the black bastard. For a spell."

"Sure as hell don't cotton to the idea much," Hyde added.

"I'm not particularly concerned whether you like it or not," Crow said, sounding casual. "All I care about is finding Luis Zambrano and getting as much of the bank's money back as we can. I need Lee Johnson. I can't afford to have you trying to kill each other before the job gets done. I made the same thing clear to Johnson. Nobody gets paid if there's any trouble between you. I want that made real clear beforehand."

It was as if a curtain fell in front of Middleton's eyes. He shook his head. "We'll leave him be, if that's the way you want it. There's always another time. Another place. He's a sneaky bastard. Better you make damn sure he understands it works both ways."

"He can add and subtract. He's no different than the two of you . . . he's only doing this for the money," Crow explained. "I'll be back in the morning with your money and your horses. We'll ride across the river and pick up Johnson; then we head west to see if we can find Zambrano's tracks. Johnson claims to know that Zambrano headquarters down around Hidalgo."

"How come you ain't lettin' us out of jail now?" Hyde asked, looking to his partner for support.

Crow turned away from the bars. "Because I don't trust you. I paid your bail and I aim to make damn sure I get my money's worth. If the two of you got in another drunken brawl tonight, Sheriff Sikes promised to lock you up and throw away the key."

Middleton's expression hardened. "If you don't trust us, how come you're takin' us along in the first place?"

"Because I need you. If I had any other choices, I'd damn sure use them."

He walked out of the jail to a dark street, swinging toward the hotel after bidding Clint Sikes a good evening. At night, the air was cooler. Limping down the boardwalk, he thought about the expedition they would launch tomorrow. He could only liken it to sitting on a powderkeg with a lighted fuse, hoping to control three dangerous men long enough to find a gang of desperados in the vast, desolate regions of northern Mexico. His plan stood only the slimmest chances of success, and yet he was still determined to attempt it. The men he was taking with him were a potentially volatile mix of bounty hunters and a wanted killer. Keeping them apart would require constant vigilance. He needed all three for the skills they possessed, but could he manage to keep them from turning on each other? The prospects were dim; yet he had no better options at the moment, and time was running short. Zambrano had a two-day head start into Mexico, and he would be spending the stolen money freely. Crow had no choice but to take the men he had and give chase. He was reminded of a time-worn old saying . . . fighting fire with fire. He would be leading a pack of killers to a rendezvous with a gang of murdering bandits. At times like this he wondered if he could be losing his mind.

He saw Tinker coming up the street from the livery, and the voice of his conscience spoke to him. The boy did not belong on a mission of the kind they were undertaking. He had no experience with hard men and raging gun battles. He'd never been to war, witnessed its terrible death scenes. His lack of experience made him the most likely candidate to catch a bullet in a fracas with Zambrano's *bandidos*. His death would be a burden Crow knew he could not bear, thus there was no real choice in the matter. Tinker had to be sent home. As badly as another gun might be needed in a showdown with Zambrano, the price would come too high if the boy lost his life over sacks of money.

"I paid the board bill on their horses like you told me," Tinker said when they met in front of the hotel. "They own a couple of crowbaits, a big bay an' a ewe-necked sorrel. Starved half to death, but they look like remount thoroughbreds with a lot of stamina."

Crow shook his head. "I've been thinking. We drove those bandits off before they could loot the mercantile of the guns and ammunition Buck kept. Never gave it another thought at the time, but we rode off and left everything in town unprotected. If that bunch doubled back to make a try for those guns, there isn't anybody to keep them from taking what they want. We've got a duty to the people of Carrizo. One of us has to go back to keep an eye on things. I'm sending you back in the morning. Bad as I need the extra gun and another pair of eyes, I've got no choice. We're sworn to protect the citizens and property in Dimmit County, and that means one of us has to be there."

There was a mixture of relief and doubt on Tinker's face. "I reckon I can handle it if they do come back, Jim Ed. We can hide Buck Davis's guns someplace where nobody'd find them. But you'll be all alone with them three hard cases. If they take the notion to kill you, won't nobody be there to stop 'em."

"That's a chance I'll have to take. Our first responsibility is to the citizens of Dimmit County. One of us has to be on the job."

"Are you right sure you ain't just sendin' me back to get me out of the way for when the shootin' starts?" Tinker asked.

"I'm sure. Like I said, I could damn sure use another gun if we run across Zambrano, but one of us has to stay to protect that stock of guns. I can take care of myself around those two bounty hunters and Lee Johnson."

"You don't sound so all-fired sure of it," the boy argued, trying to read Crow's expression in the dark. "I'd figured to go along with you. Never claimed I wasn't scared of the notion, but I was aimin' to go."

"It isn't a question of courage. You showed plenty of backbone when that gang hit town. It's the town I'm thinking about. We can't leave them to fend for themselves while we both go off on this goose chase down in Mexico. One of us has to handle the lawman's job, and it falls to you. I'm charging you with the responsibility for those guns while I'm away, and any other legal matters that arise. You'll be acting sheriff. I know you can handle it. Now let's get some sleep. It's been a long couple of days."

They entered the lamplit lobby of the hotel and climbed the stairs, Crow with some difficulty on his bad leg. At a room down a dark hallway he lit a candle to undress.

Tinker was watching him as he sat on one of the twin beds to pull off his boots.

"Sure hope this ain't the last time we see each other, Jim Ed," he said softly. "I hadn't oughta be sayin' this, maybe, but goin' after Luis Zambrano ain't the smartest idea you ever had. All the money there is ain't worth losin' the feller I admire most in the whole world."

The boy's unexpected expression of sentiment touched Crow in a way he wasn't prepared to handle. "You're talking like I'm already dead, son. Quit all that jabbering so I can get some shut-eye. You've talked so damn much my ears are starting to hurt."

He took the badge off his shirt and tucked it into the bottom of his saddlebags, then snuffed out the flame and lay back on the mattress, too exhausted to undress fully. Alone with his thoughts, he pondered the chances that he might never return to Carrizo Springs. Beginning at sunrise he would be surrounded by dangerous men who would think nothing of killing him, or each other. The only thing that would keep him alive was the promise of a sizable pay day upon their return. If by some piece of luck they were able to get their hands on some of the stolen money, his troubles would begin in earnest. All three men in his employ could be expected to turn on him for a chance at the bank loot. They would be plotting to kill him in his sleep, or when his back was turned. Thus his plan, should it happen to prove successful, would make him a target for the very same gunmen he'd hired to carry it out. Was the whole idea utter madness?

It was the alternative that was forcing his hand. He knew he simply couldn't go back to Carrizo Springs to face the townspeople without making an attempt to get their money back. He could not sit idly on the front porch of the sheriff's office while many of his friends packed up their belongings to leave town when their businesses and livestock operations failed. It wasn't in him to do nothing further about the robbery; he had a responsibility to the town, to his friends, to the families of those who gave their lives trying to defend their holdings.

He closed his eyes. His decision was made. He slept.

Chapter 9

He tied the three saddled horses and the brown pack mule to a hitching post in front of the jail, satisfied that everything was ready. During the night the pain in his leg had awakened him, and he'd taken some of the laudanum the doctor gave him. After briefly inspecting the packs on the mule to be sure the ropes were snug, he mounted the steps without noticeable pain and went into the sheriff's office.

Clint Sikes offered him coffee. "No thanks. I ate down at the hotel before I sent the boy back home."

Sikes frowned. "That don't leave anybody to watch your backside when Middleton and Hyde are behind you, besides havin' to keep an eye on Lee Johnson. Until yesterday I'd have sworn before a congregation that you had good sense, Jim Ed. Today, I ain't so sure you've got any sense at all."

Crow forced a grin. "Those gents don't worry me. My deputy is too young and inexperienced for a chore like this. Besides, it's Zambrano I'm worried about. If we find him, he's liable to have a hundred men keeping us from that money."

"There's no guarantee that the three worthless bastards you're takin' along will fight when the time comes," Sikes added. "It won't come as no surprise to me if they show you a yellow streak an' hightail it to the border. Those two back yonder are back shooters, like most bounty hunters. Bounty hunters are just about the sorriest sons of bitches on earth. I'll wager they run out on you, soon as they see there's any chance they could get their asses shot off."

"Maybe," Crow replied, sighing. "I'm gambling their greed will make them stay. I'd be obliged if you'd let them out of that cell without any more sermonizing, Clint. My mind's made up to go."

Sikes went to a desk drawer and removed a pair of heavy gun belts. He tossed them on the desk top and took down his keys. "I got a receipt for your money when I took it to the bank. It's gonna stick in my craw if I have to pay any of it to Bill and Roy before you get back . . . if you get back at all. Send a note along so I'll know things are on the square. Otherwise I'm liable to lock the bastards up again, on general principles. You'll be makin' a big mistake if you turn your back on Bill Middleton. If you ain't never learned how to sleep with one eye open, it's high time you did." He wagged his head and wore a disgusted look when he went to a gun rack to take down two shotguns; then he clumped heavily into the back room to open the cell.

Roy Hyde was the first to come into the office. Unshaven, smelling of days without benefit of bath water, he merely nodded to Crow and walked over to the desk to strap on his gun. When Bill Middleton arrived in the room, he glared at Crow with his odd pale eyes, halting a few feet away.

"Wasn't no need for you to keep us locked up last

night," he said. "Now pay us that money, like you promised. You gotta prove your word is good before me an' Roy take one more step."

Sheriff Sikes entered the office before Crow could reach into his pocket for a handful of bank notes.

"Get the hell outta my jail to do your dirty business!" he snapped, aiming a finger at Middleton's chest. "I've made it real plain before that I ain't got no use for the likes of you, so don't test my patience. I'm lettin' you out as a favor to Jim Ed Crow. If I had my way about it, you'd stay in that cell until Judge Griffin got to town."

Middleton sensed that he had the advantage. He eyed the sheriff and set his chin. "We're workin' for the law now, in case you didn't know."

Sikes glared back at the bounty hunter. "Like hell you are," he snarled, drawing his lips across his teeth. "The two of you are hirin' out your guns, plain and simple. Now get the hell out of my office before I change my mind an' toss you back in that cage. I don't like the smell in here, and it ain't got a damn thing to do with lack of soap and water."

Middleton still wore a defiant look as he turned for the desk to buckle on his gun belt. "Grab them scatterguns," he said gruffly, motioning to his partner.

Crow followed the bounty hunters out on the porch as the first rays of sunshine beamed above the eastern horizon. Clint Sikes halted in the door frame to watch Hyde and Middleton boot the shotguns to their saddles.

"Don't turn your back on these two yellow bastards," Sikes warned, when Crow hesitated near the porch steps. "Same goes for Lee Johnson. I sure as hell hope this ain't the last time I ever set eyes on you, Jim Ed. We've been friends a long time."

Crow gave what might pass for a grin. "I'm not exactly a tinhorn when it comes to handling men, Clint. I'll be okay." He waved and stepped off the porch to give the bounty hunters their money. Counting out a handful of bills, he paid Roy Hyde two hundred and fifty dollars and then gave the same to Middleton. "One of you takes the mule," he said, mounting the gray as the men pocketed their money. "Keep an eye on those packs. It's been a while since I tied a diamond hitch, and I don't trust those ropes just yet."

He reined away from the sheriff's office and started for the crossing into Nuevo Laredo, listening to the creak of saddle leather as the two men boarded their horses. Before them lay the smooth surface of the Rio Grande, and he knew that when they crossed it, they were entering Luis Zambrano's home range where they would have no friendly allies. If the *federales* learned about their mission, they would oppose them for having taken the law into their own hands on Mexican soil. Making matters worse, many local citizens would be Zambrano sympathizers in favor of the revolution. They would be surrounded by enemies in a hostile land, four men on foreign soil facing overwhelming odds. Thinking about it now, Crow questioned the wisdom of it once again. He'd never been one to take big risks, preferring caution over valor. But when he considered the alternative, riding back to Carrizo Springs to watch his friends and neighbors pack their belongings and move away, he knew what he had to do. He was duty-bound, as sheriff, to make an attempt to get the money back so his conscience would let him live in peace.

His horse entered the river, and despite the heat of a

summer morning in south Texas, a tiny chill ran down his spine.

A saddled horse stood hipshot in front of the cantina, a high-withered red roan bearing numerous brands on its flanks and shoulders. Crow wondered if the gelding had been stolen from a ranch somewhere in Texas. Flanked by Middleton and Hyde, with Hyde leading the pack mule, he rode to the cantina and reined to a halt in the middle of an empty street. At this hour, the Mexican village was still asleep.

"Where's he at?" Middleton growled impatiently, eyeing the front of the cantina. "You should have told the black bastard we ain't got all day."

Before Crow could warn the bounty hunter to keep similar remarks to himself, something moved in an early morning shadow to one side of the adobe building. Lee Johnson stepped out of the shadow with a rifle butt resting against his hip, the barrel leveled at the riders.

"He's got a gun!" Hyde shouted, clawing for the pistol at his waist.

"Hold steady!" Johnson warned, followed by an ominous click when the gun was cocked, dark muzzle aiming for Hyde's chest.

"Take it easy," Crow said quickly, lifting a palm. "Lower that rifle and explain yourself. What's the reason for drawing down on us like that? You'd damn well better have a good explanation for pulling a gun on me . . ."

Johnson's eyes were on Hyde until the bounty hunter ended his draw midway through the effort, although Hyde's hand remained frozen on his gun butt. "Jus' wanted to make real sure them two understood. I'll blow both of 'em in half if they try to collect that reward posted on me. I mean to get it said afore we go off where there ain't no witnesses. Either one of 'em goes for a gun whilst I'm around, I swear before God a'mighty I'll kill 'em both dead as pig shit."

Middleton turned an angry look toward Crow. "I done told you this nigra was a sneaky bastard. We let him get the jump on us an' now you see what happened. You'll be makin' a big mistake if he comes with us. He's liable to rob us in our sleep an' leave us all for dead."

Johnson was chuckling softly. "Them words sound mighty strange comin' from you, bounty hunter. I know for a fact you killed Cactus Jack Ward whilst he was sleepin' in his bedroll that time down at Prairie Hill. I talked to a stable hand who saw you shoot him early that mornin'."

"That's a goddamn lie!" Middleton cried. "Who the hell's gonna believe the word of a darkie anyways?"

"That's enough, boys," Crow said. He pointed to Johnson. "Lower that gun and do it now!"

Johnson's gaze strayed briefly to Crow's face. "I ain't used to takin' orders from nobody," he said.

Crow's temper went on the rise. "You'll damn sure take orders from me or you won't ride with us. Personally, I don't give a damn either way, but I won't have you aim a gun at me or any of my men while you're drawing my money. Get that through your skull, or go back inside that cantina and forget the whole thing."

"You need me," Johnson replied. "You need all the guns you can get. I want them two bounty hunters to know I'll kill 'em if they try to jump me when my back's turned."

"You've made your point," Crow growled. "The four

of us are gonna need each other in order to stay alive down here. Only a damn fool would do anything to lengthen the odds against us. If the three of you are after a big pay day, you'll do everything you can to keep things so we've got a chance to get that bank loot back."

"I say we leave the nigra here," Hyde complained, with his hand still resting on his gun.

"Nobody asked you," Crow replied, watching Johnson's trigger finger relax a little as he spoke. "If you want the other half of the money I promised you, Lee Johnson goes along and nobody makes a play against him. I want that understood."

Middleton said, "I don't trust him."

Crow sighed heavily, placing his hands on his saddle horn. "If you want the truth, I don't trust any of you, but I figure you'll do just like I say, because you want the pay I offered. All three of you can make more money working for me than you can most anyplace else. That means you take your orders from me every step of the way. First time anybody goes against an order, you're done with this outfit. If we can get that stolen money back, you stand to make a whole lot more. It's time all three of you started using your heads, boys. If we don't work together, we ain't got a chance against Zambrano."

Very slowly, Johnson lowered the rifle to his side, although his eyes continued to dart back and forth from Hyde to Middleton. "I got a right to protect myself," he said quietly. "Jus' wanted 'em to know what I'd do."

"Get mounted," Crow said, as his anger cooled. "I want you riding out front when we get upriver. There'll be the tracks of seven horses moving in a hurry. If we can pick up Zambrano's trail, it'll save us some time."

"Were's my money?" Johnson asked. "You said you was payin' half afore we pulled out."

He took the last of the bank notes and leaned out of the saddle, offering the money to Johnson. The gunman came over warily, watching Middleton and Hyde as he took his pay.

"I'll fetch my hoss," Johnson said, counting the currency on his way over to the red roan.

They rode away from the cantina in silence. Johnson took the lead. Crow indicated that he wanted Middleton in front of him; then he fell in behind the bounty hunter with Hyde bringing up the rear leading the pack mule.

At the outskirts of Nuevo Laredo, Johnson heeled his roan to a short lope. Caliche dust curled skyward from the horses' hooves as they galloped away from town, following the banks of the Rio Grande. Morning sunlight quickly warmed the horses to a sweat. The heat started to build.

Half a mile from the city, Crow allowed himself to relax. A deadly confrontation between Lee Johnson and the bounty hunters had been narrowly avoided. It was senseless to kid himself into thinking the conflict between them was over, but for now, the expedition was begun.

Soon their horses slowed to a walk. Heat waves shimmered from the dry brush around them, distorting images, breathing false movement into the daggar-shaped spines of cholla and yucca plants, the slender arms of mesquite trees blanketing the flats below the river. Away from Nuevo Laredo, they entered an empty wasteland where grass was scarce, nonexistent, save for sparse patches below the sheltering mesquite limbs where the blistering sun could not completely bake moisture from the soil. Cactus beds grew in thick clusters on both sides of a narrow trail meandering beside the river. Here and there, along the riverbank, towering cottonwoods shaded the water's edge. Desert locusts, called *chichadas* by Mexican goat herders, gave off their eerie cries which could only be likened to a scream. The sound of the locusts became a maddening chorus in the otherwise silent brushland as the horses moved steadily westward beside the river.

Single file, they followed the meandering course of the Rio Grande for an hour before Middleton slowed his horse to ride beside Crow. By the look on his face, there was something on his mind.

"Me an' Roy was talkin' last night," he began. "Had this idea that there might be a better way to get at that stolen money if we did it careful. We come up with this plan. I've been thinkin' it over an' it could work if we pulled it off just right."

"I'd like to hear it," Crow replied.

"It'll be risky. We'd have to wait until our chance came, but it makes more sense than tryin' to shoot our way into their hideout."

"Like I said, I'm ready to listen to any idea."

Middleton glanced over his shoulder. "I could use a drink of whiskey if you've got any in them packs. It's been a spell since I tasted any corn squeezin's."

Crow nodded, thinking out loud. "We'll give our horses a rest when we find some decent shade. You can tell me about your idea then, and I'll unpack the whiskey."

The bounty hunter urged his horse up the trail and settled against the cantle of his saddle, apparently satisfied, leaving Crow to wonder about his plan. Was Middleton figuring the safest way to earn the extra money he'd been promised? Or was he looking for a way to double-cross the man who was paying him and make off with everything when the right opportunity came? Crow was certain of one thing now . . . Bill Middleton was the one to watch among the men he'd hired. Of the three, he seemed the most likely to betray him.

Chapter 10

A warm breeze fluttered the cottonwood leaves above them. Off in the brush the *chichadas* screamed, feeding on scant undergrowth beneath the mesquites. Squatting on their haunches in the shade beside the river, the men passed a half-pint of Tennessee whiskey back and forth while the horses grazed and filled their bellies with water.

"I've got it figured this way," Middleton began, staring blankly across the surface of the river. "This Zambrano calls himself a revolutionary. He's raisin' an army to overthrow the government down in Mexico City, so he's hirin' as many good soldiers as he can afford. Now that he's got the money he stole from the bank, he can pay top wages for men who can shoot. There ain't an army anyplace that don't have to pay its soldiers. It ain't gonna matter to him what breed a man is, so long as he can use a gun. If we was to show up, offerin' to fight for his side if the pay was right, we could pass ourselves off as professional soldiers. If it worked, we'd be inside wherever it is that he's holed-up instead of tryin' to shoot our way in. Me and Roy talked about it. We fought for the Union, so we know a thing or two about soldierin'. If we could convince

Zambrano that we were on the level about bein' experienced soldiers, he might let us get close enough to the money without a shot bein' fired. He'd start to trust us. Right at first he's liable to be suspicious, but maybe after a spell he'd quit worryin' about us and let down his guard. If we waited until the time was right, maybe some night after most of them were asleep, we could get at the money without gettin' our heads blowed off. It all rests on Zambrano believin' that we're professional soldiers who'll fight for pay."

"Mercenaries," Crow said thoughtfully, pondering the idea. But would Zambrano, or some of his men, recognize him from the fight at Carrizo Springs? Remembering the pitched battle, hot lead was flying all over the place. He'd been hidden behind the door frame of his office during most of the shooting, except for the time he caught the bullet in his thigh. But if one of the bandits had gotten a good look at him . . .

"It won't work," Johnson said flatly, keeping his distance from the others, leaning against a cottonwood trunk. "They'll figure we're up to somethin' right off."

Middleton aimed a malevolent stare at Johnson. "What the hell would you know about playin' things smart, darkie?" he said. "Usin' brains is for white men, so keep your goddamn mouth shut unless you get asked for your opinion."

Johnson stiffened. His eyes met Middleton's, until Crow spoke up.

"That's enough between the two of you. Every man in this outfit is entitled to his opinion. I'm the one who'll decide what we do. If any of you don't like the way I call it, you can pull stakes and head back after we size things up."

Middleton was watching Crow. "You ain't gonna listen to some uppity nigra, are you? A nigra ain't got the good sense God gave a billy goat."

Crow knew it was time to set things straight between them. He stood up slowly with his hand on his .44. "Lee Johnson's a man, same as the rest of us. He can speak his piece. Before we go any further I'm making it real clear that I won't listen to talk like that. Keep those notions about darkies to yourself, Bill. Don't push me on it."

Middleton's pale eyes were fixed on Crow's face. For a time they stared at each other, until finally, the bounty hunter shrugged and looked away.

"Suit yourself on it," Middleton said. "If you get to favorin' that nigra too much, me an' Roy can make tracks back to Texas."

From the corner of his eye, Crow saw Johnson relax. "I'll think about the mercenary angle. It just might work. We'd have to play it straight as a fiddle string. If they got suspicious, we'd be up to our chins in hot water. Zambrano would have us right where he wanted us, surrounded by his own men."

Hyde stirred, leaving his haunches to take the bottle from his partner. "Wouldn't be no worse than ridin' in with guns blazin'. We'll be askin' to get killed if we try to take 'em head on."

"I damn sure won't do nothin' stupid like that," Middleton said. "Not for no amount of money. I say we pass ourselves off as soldiers for hire. If Zambrano's raisin' an army, he needs good soldiers. We can wait 'til the time is right, maybe some night when they're all asleep; then we jump the guards and make off with the money. We hightail it to the border before they know what hit 'em."

Crow could tell by Johnson's expression that he still

wasn't happy with the idea. "Until we see the lay of things, where they are and how many men Zambrano has around him, it's probably a waste of time to guess how to handle it. First thing is to find them and look the place over. It's Lee's job to track them down. When we get there, we can decide the best way to handle it."

"We're wastin' time," Johnson said, straightening beside the tree after a glance toward the surrounding brush. He ambled down to the river and caught his horse as the others came to their feet. It was then Crow noticed the handle of a knife above the top of one of Johnson's stovepipe boots.

An hour before dark, as they rode the river trail, Johnson halted his horse abruptly and swung down to study something in the caliche. He looked south, then north, to the edge of the Rio Grande. "This is where they came across," he said when Crow rode up beside him. "Seven hosses. Tracks ain't more'n a couple of days old. They headed due south through them mesquites an' they was movin' in a hurry."

To the south, rolling hills blanketed by thick brush ran to the horizon. Crow studied the hills briefly. "Let's water these horses and follow their tracks until it gets too dark to see," he said, sleeving sweat from his forehead, worn down by monotonous hours spent in a saddle. "This is liable to be the last water we find for several days."

"I'm takin' myself a bath," Hyde offered, riding up behind the others with the mule.

"Damn glad to hear it," Middleton said without intending any humor. "Every time the wind changes, my nose picks up this powerful stink."

"You ain't exactly no handful of flowers yourself," Hyde remarked dryly as he stepped down from his saddle. "This here mule has got a better smell." He unbuckled his gun belt and hung it around his saddle horn; then he trudged down to the river and waded into the shallows fully clothed while the horse and mule lowered their heads to graze.

Crow opted for a bath himself and dismounted, looping his reins over a mesquite limb before taking off his gun and shirt. Hunger rumbled in his belly when he went down to the river to pull off his boots. Moments later, Middleton and Johnson joined them in the water after hanging their weapons from their saddles and shedding their shirts, although Crow noted that Johnson still carried the knife in his boot when he waded into the shallows.

While they were in the river, Crow thought about Middleton's idea, offering their services to Zambrano as mercenaries. Off and on, he'd been thinking about it all afternoon. Should any of the bandits recognize him, he faced certain death. He tried to remember the gun battle clearly. Had any of the Mexicans ridden close enough to him during the shooting to identify him? Was it a chance he was willing to take?

He watched Johnson walk out on the riverbank and followed him to a grassy spot where he could pull on his boots. "You said you didn't think it would work, trying to pass ourselves off as mercenaries. You never did explain why . . ."

Johnson wiped himself off with his shirt, scanning the southern horizon thoughtfully. "Mexicans think different than most," he said. "They don't trust nobody 'cept themselves. If we was to show up right after they robbed a bank, they'd have to be mighty dumb not to figure why we was there. Somebody'd guess we was after the money. Wouldn't be natural for us to show up so soon after they done a robbery."

Johnson's reasoning added up, looking at things from Zambrano's side. "Maybe you're right," Crow said, sighing, fitting wet feet into boot leather. "But if we could make them believe us somehow . . ."

"We'd have to have somethin' they wanted," Johnson explained. "Guns, or ammunition for the guns they've got. There needs to be a reason for 'em to do business with us. Claimin' to be soldiers ain't gonna be enough to interest a man who's raisin' an army when he jus' robbed a bank in Texas. Four Texans show up and he'll be suspicious as hell. Liable to get us all killed in front of a firin' squad, or hung."

"We ran them out of Carrizo Springs before they could get at the guns in the mercantile," Crow remembered.

Johnson turned. "If you still got guns, you could use 'em as bait. Lure Zambrano close to the border, offerin' to sell him rifles an' cartridges. If he's aimin' to start a war, he damn sure needs guns an' bullets. Pick the right spot an' lay a trap for him."

Crow came to his feet quickly. "If we brought a wagon load of guns to the river so we could show them to him, he'd know we had the things he wants. That way, he'd bring the money when we set up the exchange. The ambush would have to be near about perfect. He'll be watching for a trap."

"I 'spect he'd bring a bunch of men with him. Four of us ain't likely to be enough unless things was laid out jus' right to start with."

Crow was thinking out loud. "My deputy could bring the guns down in a borrowed wagon. Maybe he could round up a few men who knew how to shoot. Like you said, things would have to be set up just right in order for it to work, but maybe it's the smartest way to deal with Zambrano. Make him come to us. If we've got something he wants, he'll come . . . if he don't smell a trap."

"I say it's smarter than tryin' to join up with his army. If we was to gamble wrong on the bounty hunter's idea, they could kill us all afore we could pull out, figurin' we could bring the *federales* down on them if they let us ride off. We go in there an' offer to fight for money, we could be puttin' our necks in a noose with no way out."

Crow took his gun belt down and strapped it on as he listened to Johnson's concerns. "Maybe we could send word to Zambrano when we get close to Hidalgo that our guns are for hire. Bringing down a wagon full of rifles to set an ambush for him might be awful risky. We could find ourselves up against a hundred men. The trap could backfire on us."

Johnson wagged his head. "I say those Mexicans are gonna smell a polecat if four men show up jus' after they done a bank robbery. Only thing that'll make sense to 'em is that we aim to do business with a load of guns."

Crow heard Middleton and Hyde leaving the river. "I reckon the first thing to do is find Zambrano and look things over. We can decide what to do after that. I've got some jerky and corn tortillas in one of the packs. Let's eat a bite and then see if we can follow their tracks in the dark."

A pale moon showed them the way through the brush. A narrow game trail meandered southeast among the mesquites and cactus beds. Johnson led them slowly down the tracks, wary of night-feeding rattlesnakes. At night the shrill cries of the desert locusts ceased, replaced by a welcome silence broken only by the rattle of iron-shod hooves as they crossed the low hills. Off in the distance an owl hooted softly. Much farther away, a coyote called to its mate. The land was empty, too harsh for livestock, much too dry for farming. Hardly a trace of civilization existed here, understandable to those who tried to cross it. Lack of water and blast-furnace heat weakened animals quickly, and only the most knowledgeable men could survive the desert's extremes. A few widely scattered water holes offered the only hope of making the journey, and unless someone knew how to find them by reading nature's signs, they were sure to lose their lives. Crow understood these conditions as well as most, since much of south Texas was similarly dry. Their survival depended on using their horses wisely until they reached the next source of water.

Johnson halted his roan suddenly near the crest of a hill. Almost as a reflex, Crow's hand fell to the butt of his Colt. A silence followed when Middleton stopped his horse. Then a faint buzzing noise came from the brush, a sound Crow knew all too well. He urged his gray past Middleton's gelding and rode up to the spot where Johnson sat calmly atop his mount.

"A big one," Johnson said, pointing to a dark coil blocking their path in the middle of the pale caliche trail.

Even in the moonlight Crow could easily judge the size of the serpent, the thickness of a man's arm, a twisting mass of patterned scales that spelled death for a horse or a man tossed to the ground by a frightened animal. The rattler's head rose above the coils as it watched the men. Now the buzzing sound grew louder. "Close to six feet," he said quietly. "If we give it time, it'll crawl out of the way."

Johnson wagged his head. "Goes agin' my grain to leave a snake." He swung down and drew the knife from his boot, a gleaming Bowie. Approaching the serpent, he seized the blade, and with one swift motion he sent the knife hurtling toward the rattler.

The buzzing stopped abruptly. Twisting coils writhed around the cold steel piercing the snake's body. Crow saw the serpent strike the knife handle, revealing its white underbelly in a last futile attempt to kill the thing embedded in its back.

Johnson chuckled softly. "This one won't get the chance to poison good hosses. Makes one less thing we have to worry with." He walked forward until he came perilously close to the deadly fangs. Timing his next move carefully, he stepped on the rattler's head and pulled his knife from the ground; then he cut off the serpent's head and wiped the blade clean on his boot top.

While Crow was watching the affair, he paid particular attention to the sureness of Johnson's moves, more convinced than ever that among the men he'd hired for the expedition, Lee Johnson was by far the most dangerous.

Chapter 11

Off to the south and west, as dawn brightened the sky, they could see the distant outline of a mountain range. Deep in those mountains, they would come to Hidalgo. Pushing weary horses down a seldom used wagon trail, they entered a broad plain stretching to foothills below the barren, rocky slopes. A layer of chalky dust covered animals and men after a night-long ride, and now the horses' flanks were drawn, evidence of the need for water. The geldings needed rest more desperately than the sleepy-eyed men aboard their backs. Soon the heat would start to build, and conditions for the animals would only worsen.

Crow called a halt at a small thicket of taller mesquites where their mounts would have some meager shade and grazing. "Let's rest these horses a spell," he said, swinging a leg over the gray's rump to dismount.

"This is the emptiest goddamn place I ever saw," Hyde said when he was down from his sorrel. "We ain't seen a soul since we left the river."

"That's why Zambrano comes this way, I reckon," Crow replied, looping his reins around the saddle horn so his gelding could reach sun-dried tufts of buffalo grass. "Nobody sees which way he rides to hide from the *federales*. Back in those mountains yonder is Hidalgo. Been there once, a long time ago. Best I remember it's a little pueblo . . . maybe a hundred folks who tend goat herds. There's this adobe wall around the village, which makes sense if Zambrano ever has to defend himself against the *federales*. The people who live there are Yaquis. Some of the prettiest women I ever saw, too. They make damned decent *pulque*, if you can drink the stuff. Worst headache I ever had in my life was down at Hidalgo that time."

"How much farther is it?" Middleton asked, working the stiffness from his legs.

"Another day. Maybe two. Can't say as I remember exactly."

Johnson was staring at the mountains when he spoke. "I overheard some talk at the cantina in Laredo that Zambrano camps close to Hidalgo, so we'd be smart to ride real careful once we get in those mountains. The tracks are real plain so far, but there's no tellin' how long they'll stay that way when we hit those rocky climbs. If he's worried 'bout bein' followed, he'll try to hide his trail sooner or later. He's liable to have lookouts, too. Back in Nuevo Laredo, folks claim he's some kinda hero amongst the poor people in this neck of the woods. Soon as anybody spots us down here, they'll likely send word to him."

Crow removed a canteen from one of the packs and passed it to Middleton. "That's the way I've got it figured, too. This place will be full of Zambrano sympathizers. If we can find his hideout before he finds us, we'll have a chance to look things over and make up our minds about how to handle it."

"I still say it'd be smarter to ride right in and tell him

we've got guns for hire," Middleton said. "It's the only way we'll ever get close enough to get our hands on that money without startin' a war we can't win."

Johnson glanced over his shoulder. "It's the only sure way to get ourselves killed," he said thickly. "Zambrano ain't gonna be nobody's fool."

Middleton made a face; then he lifted the canteen and took a few spare swallows. Crow turned to the mountains, rubbing his chin, trying to put aside the fatigue brought on by a day and a night in the saddle.

"We'll have to cross this brushy flat before we have any hope of finding water. Sure ain't looking forward to another day on the back of this horse before we can get some sleep."

"A man can't sleep in this heat anyways," Johnson said, squinting in the sun's early glare to look south. "Might as well be miserable travelin' . . ."

The old wagon road rose and fell when it entered the foothills, and for a distance, it skirted the closest mountains by taking a southwesterly direction. Johnson rode out front, his face aimed at the ground to read the hoofprints. Crow watched the rocky slopes with a vague recollection of his visit to Hidalgo almost a decade earlier, not long after he first came to Carrizo Springs to take the job of sheriff.

Wherever the land allowed it, Johnson led them in a slow trot that was easy on the horses while still making good time. Their geldings now traveled with heads lowered, near the end of their ability to move without rest and water. Hyde's gelding had begun to cough as they were crossing the flats earlier in the day, and any experienced horseman understood what the coughing meant. Unless the animal was given water soon it would lie down to die.

Now, as the sun slanted to the west, there was sign of a spring near the base of a mountain. Standing stark against slabs of sandstone where the slope began, a tiny knot of trees held promise of a seep pool. The road ran toward the spring as Crow knew it must, for no travelers moving across this dry land could afford to miss the chance to take on water. Zambrano and his bandits had known to come this way, for the tracks continued plainly along the ruts.

As they neared the stunted cottonwoods, Johnson showed more caution. He drew his pistol and slowed the roan to a walk. When Middleton saw this he pulled his Colt, then cast a worried glance back at Crow.

"You reckon he saw somethin' in them trees?"

"I figure he's just being careful," Crow replied, although he also took out his gun when they were less than three hundred yards from the cottonwood grove.

They rode up to a small pool encircled by slender trees. The horses had to be restrained the last few yards when they scented water, fighting a pull on the curb chain to keep them from galloping the last few steps. The pack mule was last to drop its head to the surface of the pool, and while the animals were drinking, Crow swung down tiredly to examine tracks in the soft mud at the edge of the water. Among the hundreds of deer and javelina prints, some old, some recent, he saw impressions left by horses. Johnson knelt beside one of the prints to trace a fingertip around the edge.

"A couple of days," he said. He looked up the mountain. "From here on, they'll start bein' real careful. If they're worried 'bout bein' followed, they'll try to hide their tracks. It's my notion that we ride to some high ground every now an' then to see what's in front of us, so we don't ride blind."

Crow stretched aching muscles and nodded. "I've got some army field glasses in the packs. One of us can ride ahead in the morning to make sure the way is clear. Best I recall it's one more day to Hidalgo. Zambrano could be holed-up most any place around here . . . maybe in the village, if he feels safe. I'm guessing he'll be close by. A bunch of men will need food, and whiskey. Women, too. I'll lay odds he won't be far from town."

"If he's still there," Johnson remarked after a moment of thoughtful silence. "Now that he's got plenty of money, he may go lookin' for more soldiers to hire."

"If that's the case, then we'll follow him. I won't give up easy. That money belongs to my friends."

Johnson seemed amused. "Never did hear of no lawman so all-fired dedicated to his job."

Crow thought about what the gunman said. "I wouldn't call it dedication to a job, although maybe that's a part of it. I owe it to the families to do as much as I can to get their life savings back. I reckon you could say I'm doing it out of friendship, rather than dedication. Hardly anyone around Carrizo Springs can shoot straight, so that don't leave anybody else besides me to go after the money."

Middleton and Hyde came over to look at the hoof-prints.

"We gotta get some shut-eye," Middleton said. "I damn near fell asleep in the saddle a while ago."

Crow tented his shoulders and took a deep breath. "We'll toss our bedrolls here until sunup. Boil some coffee and eat a little fatback. Those horses aren't able to travel now anyway. Pretty soon this road will start climbing and our mounts need to be fresh."

"How about some more of that whiskey?" Hyde asked, passing his tongue across sun-cracked lips. "We could all use a drink to take our minds off our saddle sores."

"Let's pull our gear and get a fire going as soon as our horses are full. I could use some whiskey myself. Can't remember when I've ever been so tired . . ."

Plodding about on leaden legs, Crow gathered mesquite limbs for firewood while the others unsaddled horses and removed the packs from the mule. In the shelter of cottonwood branches he built a small fire and put coffee on to boil. Every now and then he glanced to the mountains, nagged by the vague feeling that someone was watching them now.

Middleton was examining one of the rifles Crow had purchased in Laredo when he came over to the packs to look for a fresh bottle of whiskey.

"Winchester model '73," Crow said. "I figured we'd need them if we got in a showdown with Zambrano. Sheriff Sikes told me you and your partner didn't own a long gun."

Middleton wore a sour expression. "We fell on some hard times up in San Antone, so we sold our rifles. There's times when the manhuntin' trade ain't so good. Me an' Roy was needin' a pay day about the time you showed up."

Crow uncorked the bottle and took a healthy swallow; then he sighed and drew a forearm across his mouth, handing the whiskey to Middleton. "With a bit of luck this could be a good-sized pay day. Depends on what we find when we locate Zambrano."

Hyde trudged over, finished with hobbling the horses

and mule, just as Middleton drank deeply. "Hand me that jug afore I choke," he said, scratching his dark beard stubble. "Maybe we oughta pass around them Winchesters, now that we're gettin' close to that bunch of Mexicans."

"Take one," Crow offered, "and a box of shells. From here on out I figure we need to be ready for trouble."

Hyde removed a rifle from the canvas sling and started to load it after swallowing a mouthful of whiskey. Crow was watching Johnson, puzzled by the gunman's behavior. Johnson stood at the edge of the cottonwood grove, gazing south as if he'd seen something off in the distance.

"Wonder what he's looking at," Crow murmured.

Johnson heard the sheriff and turned around. "We got ourselves some company. Yonder, on the side of that mountain. You can't see 'em now, but there was something movin' up there. Looked like two fellers on foot. Too far to be sure, but I'd nearly swear I saw two of 'em."

"I never saw nobody," Hyde argued, scanning the slopes.

"They was there," Johnson said quietly, sounding sure of it.

Crow stood up and walked over to the edge of the trees. "I had this feeling a while ago that we were being watched, like something was crawling down the back of my neck." He recalled what Clint Sikes had told him, that Johnson had done some scouting for the army during the Indian wars; thus his instincts would be good.

"It means Zambrano will know we're here," Johnson said. "If he's camped close by, whoever is watchin' us will tell him."

"I'll get those field glasses," Crow said, still eyeing the

mountain. "Maybe you can spot them before it gets dark."

When he had given Johnson the binoculars, he set about to fry salt pork at the fire. Sleep weighted his eyelids, yet he kept glancing to the south where Johnson had seen movement. Dusk purpled the slopes and the brush around the spring before the fatback was cooked. Johnson remained frozen in the shadows below the trees, sweeping the field glasses over the mountains.

Hyde and Middleton came to the fire with their bedrolls. The smell of fried meat and coffee soon caught Johnson's attention, and he left the edge of the grove to join them for supper.

"See anything?" Crow asked, placing strips of bacon in a tortilla.

"Not since the first time. If I had to guess, I'd say they hightailed it to Zambrano with the news somebody is following him. We could have ourselves some company afore mornin'."

Crow carried his food to the edge of the trees, gazing up the face of the mountain towering above them. Darkness covered the silent peaks farther to the south.

This is where it all starts, he thought. It's too late to turn back now.

He heard soft footfalls behind him. Johnson walked to a cottonwood trunk and leaned against it, chewing his supper.

"Maybe it's time you made up your mind what you're gonna say to Zambrano if he shows up. I don't figure it'll be long 'til we get a look at him face-to-face. He'll be watchin' us from now on. The closer we get to him, the more he's gonna wonder about us."

"I haven't decided just yet. If you guessed right, that he

already knows we're here, then I reckon I'd better come up with a story. I'd hoped to slip up on him first, to look things over."

Chewing a mouthful of food, the gunman glanced up at the sky thoughtfully. "It's hard to slip up on a man who's expectin' trouble. I say if we promise him a shipment of guns for a fair price, he'll gamble some. He needs rifles and ammunition to win a revolution. He may not trust us, but he'll do business with the devil hisself to get what he wants."

Crow wondered about it. Could a dangerous border bandit be lured close to the Rio Grande to buy rifles? Would Zambrano ride into an ambush carrying the money stolen from Carrizo Springs? "I'll sleep on it," he said. "One of us needs to take the first watch, just in case somebody decides to try to kill us in our bedrolls or steal our horses."

"I'll take the first watch," Johnson said. "Seein' those two fellers a while ago woke me up right smart. I'll come fetch you around midnight. It'd be my suggestion we douse that fire right away. No reason to make it easy for 'em if they decide to come pay us a call."

Chapter 12

Dawn grayed the sky, faintly illuminating the slopes. Crow sat with his back against a cottonwood trunk watching pale light creep across the mountains. The night had passed without incident, and he felt better after a few hours of sleep. Keeping watch, he had toyed with a number of ideas until sunrise, ways to approach the bandits if they encountered them unexpectedly on the ride to Hidalgo. Convincing Zambrano that they meant him no harm would be tricky. The story they told him would have to be good.

Someone stirred in the grove behind him. Moments later Lee Johnson came to the edge of the trees, buckling on his gun belt.

"All's quiet," Crow said, climbing to his feet.

Johnson stared at the mountains. "Maybe too quiet," he replied softly, scanning the brush around them now. "No birds comin' to water. Something's out there . . . I can feel it in my bones."

Crow examined the brush surrounding their campsite briefly. "Maybe you're being too superstitious, Lee. I'm sure I'd have seen something if anybody tried to sneak up on us."

"Got nothin' to do with superstition. There ain't no birds comin' to drink. No deer or wild pigs either. Somethin' has got the wild animals scared off. This is likely the only water for miles. It ain't natural for things to be so still . . . so quiet."

"It's us," Crow argued, although now he was growing edgy himself. "Our horses and the four of us have got the birds spooked away. It's our smell, maybe."

"I still say it's too quiet out there. Nothin' moving at all."

"I'll wake the others up," Crow said uneasily. "Time we got a move on anyway, now that it's light."

Johnson nodded. "I wouldn't build no fire just now. Our smoke could be seen from a long way off. No reason to advertise the fact that we're here if they don't already know."

Crow hurried to awaken Middleton and Hyde, filled with a sense of foreboding. Could Johnson be right? Was someone out in the brush watching them now?

He woke the two bounty hunters and then moved quickly to bring in the horses and mule for saddling while continually keeping an eye on the brushlands around the spring.

The road climbed sharply, angling across switchbacks to provide the gentlest grade. There was total silence all around them, broken only by the clatter of horseshoes. Johnson led them up the mountain, pausing often to examine the trail ahead very carefully before continuing the ascent. Something was worrying the gunman.

At the top of a steep grade Johnson halted his roan to study the slopes with field glasses. For a time he sat motionless, and the delay began to wear away on Crow's nerves. He heeled the gray forward and rode to the crest where Johnson waited.

"See anything?" he asked when the gelding came to a halt.

For several seconds he got no answer; then Johnson lowered the binoculars and shook his head.

"It's what I don't see that's got me worried," Johnson said. "There ain't a damn thing movin' up yonder. No sparrows in any of the bushes, like somethin' already scared them away. Only one way to explain it. We're bein' watched. Whoever it is, they're keepin' out of sight and stayin' ahead of us to see where we aim to go."

"You sound mighty damn sure of it," Crow said.

"Trackin' Apaches taught me a thing or two. An Injun can move mighty quiet most times, but even Apaches can't move around without scarin' off wild birds. Somebody's keepin' an eye on us since we got to that spring last night. Got the feelin' real strong just now."

"We could be riding into an ambush," Crow said.

"Not if I can help it," Johnson replied, urging his roan to a walk over the top of the rise.

Below, a yawning canyon ran between two rugged peaks. Rock lay clustered along the canyon floor. In places, the gorge was narrow, perfect spots for a bushwhacking.

"I don't like the looks of this," Middleton said, turning back in the saddle.

"Neither do I," Crow said, following the faint wagon road with his eyes. "We could get caught in a cross fire . . ."

Where the road climbed again beyond the twin mountains, he saw a sharp bend in the trail, a turn to the southwest where the ruts went out of sight. Riding out of the gorge, they would be forced to approach the bend without an escape route, trapped inside walls of stone that would make them easy pickings for sharpshooters on either side. A cold sweat started to form on Crow's forehead. Were they headed into a trap?

He sent the gray into a trot and rode past Middleton. As he neared the front of the procession, Johnson glanced over his shoulder and abruptly stopped his horse to wait for Crow.

"Yonder's where they're most likely to bushwhack us, Lee. I say we look for another way around."

"Been thinkin' the same thing," Johnson said, frowning at the pass. "I was aimin' to climb one side on foot to make sure the way is clear. When I give the signal, the rest of you can ride on through." He reached for a boot below one stirrup leather and drew out his rifle, a large-bore Remington rolling block carbine with a muzzle the size of a man's thumb. "If there's anybody up there, I can shoot plumb across the canyon with this," he added.

Crow sleeved the clamy sweat from his face. "I reckon we oughta try it. It could take half a day to find another way around. If any shooting starts, get down as quick as you can. I'll be holding your horse out of range."

Johnson gave him a half smile. "I trust you, lawman. If I didn't, I damn sure wouldn't hand over the reins to this here hoss way off in the middle of nowhere. A man without a hoss in this god-forsaken place is the same as dead. Never trusted no lawman afore today. Can't say jus' why you're different . . ."

"Lead the way," Crow said, eyeing the canyon walls.

"When you find a place where you can scale that rock, say the word."

They entered the gorge at a walk. Crow rode behind Johnson now, resting the butt plate of his Winchester on his thigh as he scanned the cliffs above them. The echo of iron horseshoes was magnified, trapped inside walls of stone.

For the first quarter mile they descended into the belly of the canyon. Johnson rode cautiously, pausing frequently to study the mountains on either side. Reaching level ground, they made another slow hundred yards before the road began a gradual climb toward the narrow pass at the top. Then, near a pile of boulders fallen from one of the slopes, Johnson halted his roan and dismounted with the rifle.

"I'll wave my hat if there ain't nobody waitin' for us 'round that turn," he said, handing Crow his reins. "These here rocks will give you some cover if they start pourin' lead down on us." He wheeled for a ledge running up the rock face and began to climb the side of the mountain.

Crow watched the gunman's agile footwork on the ledge. He had unusual grace for a muscular man. Johnson seemed to scale the cliff effortlessly, as though he'd done it a hundred times before. A few minutes later he went out of sight over the lip of a sandstone abutment.

"That damn nigra can climb like a goat," Middleton said. "I sure as hell hope he can shoot if there's anything up there."

"I'll wager he's a good shot," Crow replied. "I've run across plenty of men I'd rather be facing in a shooting contest."

Middleton grunted. "How come you're so all-fired soft

on that darkie?" he asked. "You sound like a Southerner to me."

Crow let out a sigh, still watching the side of the mountain. "Never did care much what color a man's skin was, to tell the truth. I was too young to understand what we were fighting over when I went off to the war. Folks claimed it was something called states' rights. Never knew exactly what it was back then."

"You're makin' a mistake by trustin' that nigra. He's a killer with a price on his head."

"I've got something he wants," Crow said evenly. "Until he can get his hands on the money I promised him, he'll do everything he can to keep us alive. Fact is, the same goes for you and your partner. Without me there's no pay day for any of you."

"Me an' Roy can be trusted," Middleton protested. "Hell, we've always worked on the side of the law——"

A sudden explosion near the top of the pass ended the bounty hunter's remark. In the same instant, Crow and Middleton were shouldering their rifles. The shot spooked their horses, and for a time the animals needed settling before the echo of the gunshot faded.

"Ride for those rocks!" Crow shouted, wheeling his gray for the boulders west of the road when he found no target for the Winchester. Amid the rattle of horseshoes, they rode for the rock pile as fast as they could and jerked their horses to a halt.

Crow peered above the boulders, standing in his stirrups for a view of the trail and the ledge where Johnson had begun his climb. Following the roar of the gun, there was silence. "Just that one shot," he whispered to himself, puzzled by the absence of answering fire. He knew the lone gunshot had come from the big Remington by the heavy sound of the explosion.

"How come ain't nobody else shootin'?" Hyde asked, cradling the Winchester in the crook of his arm.

"Hard to say," Crow answered when the quiet lingered.

"I say that damn nigra got jumpy, maybe," Middleton said, watching the slopes above them. "His itchy trigger finger is gonna announce the fact that we're here, damn his worthless black hide."

Crow didn't bother with speculation just then, as his gaze wandered back and forth across the top of the pass. He felt the gray relax underneath him. "Wish the hell we knew what he was shooting at," he muttered to himself.

A full minute later, when it seemed the silence would last, a gun roared. Three answering shots followed in rapid succession, and the whine of speeding lead echoed from the bend.

"They're coming for him!" Crow shouted, kicking his right boot from the stirrup to jump from the saddle. "They're gonna rush him! Hold these horses!"

Middleton swung down before Crow could start up the gorge. "I'm comin' with you," he said, tossing Hyde the reins on his bay.

Crow was set to offer argument when a staccato of gunfire erupted from the pass. Middleton ran past him clutching the Winchester. Then the heavier thud of Johnson's Remington added its voice to the battle sounds, and there was no time to consider who would go and who would stay. Crow took off behind the bounty hunter, running in a low crouch, listening to the chatter of rifles.

Middleton reached the ledge where Johnson had begun his climb and scrambled up the rock face. Quickly out of breath, Crow was panting when he started up the narrow trail. There was a momentary pause in the shooting. Middleton stumbled and fell to one knee. Before he regained his feet there was a distant gunshot, followed by the much closer bellow of Johnson's rifle, and a shrill scream of pain from the far side of the pass.

Middleton reached a level spot and hesitated, hunkered down with the rifle to his shoulder. Crow hurried up the trail and halted beside him, gasping for air, trying to see what made the bounty hunter cautious.

"Over yonder," Middleton whispered, pointing to a spot across the gorge. "Too far to make a sure shot. Have to get closer—"

The roar of Johnson's Remington drowned out the last words to leave Middleton's mouth. On the far side of the pass a man pitched forward, clutching his chest as he toppled off the rim and plummeted downward, uttering a garbled cry.

"Sweet Jesus," Middleton said softly, watching the body tumble out of sight. "That was one hell of a shot . . . musta been nigh onto four hundred yards."

Guns pounded from half a dozen places among the rocks across the pass, and in the same instant, Crow and Middleton were running in a low crouch toward a rock slide where the level spot ended. A slug ricocheted off the mountainside above them, and Crow dove for the ground with his heart hammering inside his chest.

Chapter 13

Lee Johnson was somewhere above them, higher up the mountain. When he fired, the report from his rifle hinted at his location, and yet Crow could only guess where he was, for they were blinded by a turn in the rock face. Middleton lay behind a cluster of rock fallen from the mountain, peering over the top of the stones. Crow chose a position at the edge of the rimrock with a view of the bottom of the pass. For now, he found nothing to shoot at.

A rifle cracked from the far side of the bend. The slug struck the rock pile where Middleton was hiding, making a dull whacking noise that sent the bounty hunter ducking for cover.

"I can't see the bastards," Middleton growled, risking a look over the rocks again, sweeping his rifle sights back and forth aimlessly.

"Neither can I," Crow said in the following silence. He was sweating profusely now. "If we can get off this ledge, maybe we can work our way around—"

Johnson's carbine thundered. Somewhere across the pass, a muffled cry sounded. Two answering shots came from the rim of the bend; Crow saw a pair of brief muzzle flashes, one from a yucca plant where he quickly trained his Winchester. Steadying the gun against his shoulder, he squeezed the trigger gently and felt the rifle kick, accompanied by the roar of exploding gunpowder.

The yucca moved, changing shape before his eyes when it shed some of its daggarlike spines. As Crow was levering the empty shell from the chamber, Middleton fired. A puff of chalky dust arose from the edge of the distant cliff.

"Damn," Middleton hissed through clenched teeth. "Missed the son of a bitch by a country mile. I'll hand it to that darkie . . . he can damn sure shoot. Maybe it's that rifle."

Suddenly more guns crackled from the far side of the pass, and the air above them was full of whistling lead. Stray bullets struck the mountain above them from every angle, making a singsong whine. Crow pressed flat against the rock with his eyes closed until the volley died down to an occasional shot.

"Son of a bitch!" Middleton exclaimed, inching backward. "I swear there's fifty of the bastards shootin' at us now. If we stay here, they'll fill us full of holes. I'm goin' back to the horses—if I can get there in one piece."

"What about Lee? He's up there all by his lonesome!"

"To hell with him. He was dumb enough to go in the first place. Right now I'm lookin' out for my own skin. The nigra's on his own."

Before Crow could argue the point, Middleton was off in a running crouch for the trail. Several gunshots popped in the distance, but the bullets went high and wide of their mark, some bouncing harmlessly off the face of the slope until the bounty hunter went out of sight.

Crow risked a look across the pass, lifting his head only slightly when the shooting stopped until he heard the scrape of a boot somewhere above him. He saw Johnson running along a narrow slice in the rock, bent over to present as small a target as possible. Seconds later a hail of molten lead splattered all around the spot amid the concussion from dozens of rifles just as Johnson dove for the ground.

He's dead, Crow thought. There's no way he could have escaped all those bullets.

Wriggling back from the rim, Crow judged his own chances of making the trail before he met a similar fate. He scrambled to his hands and knees with a knot of fear growing in his belly and a cottony taste in his mouth. As he was preparing to make a desperate lunge away from the rimrock, a booming gunshot came from the spot where Johnson went down, then the metallic tinkle of an empty cartridge rattled down the side of the mountain.

"Run!" a voice cried from above.

Without thinking Crow took off in a stumbling run, holding his rifle against his ribs. Behind him, guns chattered. A slug plowed a tiny furrow near his feet and he ran faster, feeling like his chest would explode from fear and exertion. He raced thirty yards to the mouth of the trail and jumped as though he'd sprouted wings. Tumbling, he landed on his chest and heard himself grunt above the crackle of gunfire. Lead whistled over him for a few seconds more, and then the shooting stopped. He found he was lying facedown on the narrow game trail. A few inches to the right and he would have fallen down the side of the gorge.

His head cleared suddenly and he remembered Johnson. He pushed himself up on his hands and knees and picked up the rifle before making a careful turn to crawl back to the top of the trail. In the slice where he'd seen the gunman fall, sunlight glinted off the barrel of a rifle.

"I'll try to cover you!" he shouted, raising the Winchester to his shoulder. "Soon as I start shooting, make a run for it!"

Without waiting for a reply, he sighted across the pass and nudged the trigger, levering another shell before the gun blast ended. He fired again, and a third time, chambering fresh cartridges as quickly as he could. From the corner of his eye he saw Johnson jump from the niche. On the far side of the bend, guns began to pop. Crow fired until his rifle was empty, and when he heard the dull click of the hammer, he drew back to be out of harm's way.

A fast-moving figure darted back and forth across the ledge. Johnson dove to his stomach and did a hurried belly crawl to the top of the trail, his face a mask of determination. He fell over the lip and lay there panting, arms and legs trembling.

"That was mighty close," he gasped. "Let's get to them hosses afore they circle 'round behind us. There's way too damn many of 'em for us to keep up this here fight."

The gunfire ended as they started down the ledge to the bottom of the gorge. A hundred yards away, Crow could see the rocks where their horses were hidden. Before they reached level ground both of them were running toward the boulders, when a sight beyond the rocks caused them to pull up short.

No fewer than twenty mounted men came down the gorge from the north, riding their horses at an easy trot. They were spread out in a ragged line to prevent any chance of escape. Crow saw the heavy cartridge belts across their chests, the bearded faces beneath the shadows of dusty sombreros, rifles and pistols aimed at the men trapped in the pass.

"We're finished," Crow said softly, lowering the muzzle of his empty Winchester. "Unless we can do some tall talking, we're the same as dead. They've got us cold . . ."

Behind the boulders, Middleton and Hyde sat their horses with their hands in the air, surrendering without a fight in the face of overwhelming odds. Johnson took a deep breath and then lowered his rifle. "Tell 'em we got guns to sell," he whispered. "That'll be jus' about the onliest reason they'll let us live."

Crow started off to meet the advancing riders on unsteady legs, exhausted by their ordeal and close brushes with death, weighted down by a feeling of hopelessness. His plan to retrieve the stolen bank loot seemed doomed to failure, and it now appeared he would lose his life in the process. With the best of intentions, he had set out on an impossible quest against the advice of the Laredo sheriff. Too, he had seriously misjudged the determination of his adversaries, and their cunning. He'd led his men into a trap from which there was no escape . . . unless he could convince the Mexicans there was ample reason to let them live.

Riding at the front of the group, a lanky *pistolero* said something Crow couldn't hear and pointed to him. As Crow trudged past the boulders where Hyde and Middleton were watching the riders with arms lifted high above their heads, Middleton spoke.

"It's up to you to save our asses . . . better make it a pretty speech, or we're fishbait."

Crow ignored the remark and strode toward the leader, all the while wondering if any of the Mexicans could identify him from the bank robbery at Carrizo Springs. A quick glance around the bunch revealed that Zambrano wasn't with them now.

He halted a few yards from the slender *pistolero's* horse and thumbed his hat back. At a signal from their leader, the other Mexicans stopped their mounts. To make a show of a peaceful surrender, Crow dropped his Winchester to the ground and lifted his hands.

"We're looking for Luis Zambrano," Crow began. "From the looks of things, I reckon we just found him. It wasn't our idea to start all this shooting. We aimed to talk business, only we didn't get the chance. Your men started shooting at us."

The lanky Mexican looked him up and down, his dark eyes hooded with suspicion. "What business you have with Luis?" he asked in thickly accented English.

"Guns. Repeating rifles. We've got some Winchester '73s to sell, and we heard Zambrano might be interested."

The *pistolero* was still wary. "Where are these rifles? I see only one mule . . ."

Crow heard sounds coming from the pass behind him, and he glanced over his shoulder. Dozens of cotton-clad men in straw sombreros cradling rifles now filled the mouth of the bend. "We have them across the border near Laredo. A wagon full of Winchesters and ammunition. But first, we've got to talk to Zambrano and discuss the price."

"I am Capitan Julio Cortez. Who are you?"

Crow swallowed uncomfortably. "Why are names important? Selling guns in Mexico is against the law back in Texas. My name shouldn't matter if I can furnish you with rifles."

Cortez scowled; then he raised the rifle resting on the

pommel of his saddle and aimed it down at Crow's chest. "I ask you for a name, señor. Perhaps only so it can be carved on your tombstone. Tell me who you are, if you value your life."

"My name is Smith. I'm a gun dealer."

"So you say, señor," Cortez replied. "But I see no guns. Why should I believe you? Tell me why I should not have you killed, Tejano."

"Because you need rifles for the revolution, and we've got them. Plenty of cartridges, too. You can't buy them across the border unless you deal with someone like me. I'm after a profit and you need guns to fight the *federales*. If Luis Zambrano has the money, we can deliver the rifles and ammunition."

Cortez regarded Crow for a moment, giving the sheriff a chance to briefly examine the guns the Mexicans carried. Most of their rifles were old carbines, Spencers and Sharps. Zambrano's men needed weapons if they meant to fight a well-equipped Mexican army.

"What is the price for these Winchesters?" Cortez asked.

"That'll depend on several things. If you come to the border and pick them up close to the river, they'll be cheaper. The four of us ain't looking for the chance to dodge *federale* patrols. Also depends on the kind of money you spend. If you've got American dollars, it'll fetch you the best price. Too many *pesos* will arouse suspicion back in Texas. There'll be too many questions."

Cortez's horse stamped a hoof to rid its leg of a fly. The heat at the bottom of the gorge became unbearable. Sweat trickled down Crow's back, plastering his shirt to his skin. Beads of sweat rolled down from his hat band into his eyes. All the while, Cortez watched him warily, as though he doubted Crow's story about the rifles.

"How did you know where to find us?" Cortez asked as his eyelids slitted again.

"We heard talk at a cantina in Nuevo Laredo that Zambrano had a camp close to Hidalgo. It was a long shot, but with guns to sell I decided to try it."

Now Cortez gave him a mirthless grin. "How do we know you have not led the *federales* to this place?"

"That's easy enough. Send someone to scout our trail, and you'll see we came alone. Nobody is following us. You've got my word on it."

At that, Cortez laughed. "Why should we take the word of a Tejano who freely admits he will break the law to sell us guns?"

Crow shifted his weight to the other foot, noticing that Cortez lowered his rifle. "I reckon you'll take my word because you need me. You need the guns and cartridges I can sell you."

"Perhaps," Cortez replied. "But first, we will see if you are telling the truth. I will send some men to see if anyone is following you. Tell the other *Tejanos* to remove their gun belts and place all their weapons in a pile. I was prepared to give the order to have you killed, Señor Smith. For now, your lives will be spared until I am sure you came here alone." He turned to one of his men and spoke rapidly in Spanish; then his gaze fell on Lee Johnson as three Mexicans wheeled their horses to ride back through the gorge. *"El negro* is a fine marksman. I saw him shoot accurately across a great distance. I am curious to see the rifle he carries."

"His name's Lee Johnson. Him and the other two are experienced soldiers. If the pay was right, we might consider doing some fighting for your side in this revolution."

"Ah, *los mercenarios,*" Cortez said, glancing at the two bounty hunters. "If you are telling the truth about coming alone, perhaps *el jefe* will discuss this matter with you. It is not for me to say what Luis will do, for I am only a lowly *capitan* in his army."

"You'll see I'm telling the truth. We've got as much to lose as you do if the *federales* find us."

"Tell your men to remove their guns, señor. My *soldados* will return before dark. Until then, you are my prisoners. If any of you try something foolish, I can promise you a speedy death."

Chapter 14

Resting in the shade below a towering sandstone cliff, Crow sat on his haunches between Middleton and Johnson, speaking very softly. Cortez's soldiers held a loose circle around them now, idling away the afternoon beside their horses.

"Captain Cortez seemed interested," Crow remembered. "I told him we'd do some fighting for his side if the price was right. He says that isn't up to him. Zambrano makes all the decisions."

Roy Hyde stirred atop his bedroll behind them. Until now he'd been dozing with his hat over his face. "Makes me edgy," he said, "bein' without a gun while we do all this waitin'. Feels like I'm damn near naked."

"Cortez is just being careful," Crow said.

Johnson squinted in the sun's bright glare when he looked around them. "They're damn sure a rough-lookin' bunch, most of 'em. If things don't go jus' right, they'll kill every last one of us. We've got to make 'em believe we've got those rifles. That's the only way we'll get out of this mess alive."

Middleton frowned. "We stand a chance of gettin' hired as paid soldiers, in my estimation."

"It's the guns they want," Johnson insisted. "Most of 'em are carryin' single-shot rifles. With repeaters they can shoot seven times."

Crow was watching Julio Cortez. The captain was seated in the shade, talking quietly with some of his men. Now and then he cast a look in Crow's direction. "Cortez ain't quite sure what to do with us. When he knows our backtrail is clear, I think he'll take us to Zambrano."

At dusk, as Crow and his men dozed in the shadow below the cliff, the three soldiers returned on lathered horses. Crow heard distant hoofbeats and came wide awake. "They're back," he whispered, nudging Middleton with an elbow.

The bounty hunter sat up to rub his eyes. "Seems like I've been a prisoner ever since me an' Roy came to Texas. First that goddamn Laredo jail, and now we're surrounded by Mexican revolutionaries who'd like to put us before a firing squad. Things got pretty wild up in Kansas a time or two, but never as bad as this. Abilene an' Dodge City seem kinda tame by comparison."

Johnson took his hat off his face to watch the riders come down the gorge. "I counted sixty men with Cortez. Even if we find out where they're keepin' that money, we ain't got much of a chance of gettin' our hands on it without a hell of a fight."

"If they buy our story, we'll have some time to look things over," Crow said, watching the three soldiers dismount in front of Cortez. "If you take a close look at most of these men, you can tell they ain't had much experience with a gun. They're simple farmers who believe in Zambrano's revolutionary cause. I count about a dozen who look like they can handle themselves."

"I was jus' thinkin' the same thing," Johnson said, passing a glance over the men around Cortez. "The owlhoots wearin' gun belts figure to know a thing or two, but the rest look like *peons*. Most of 'em ain't even got horses."

Cortez directed a look at Crow; then he started toward them flanked by several soldiers. He wore a flat expression that gave no hint of his intentions before he arrived. Spurs rattled over the rock and came to a halt. Cortez gave Crow a piercing stare.

"My *soldados* say no one is following you. Perhaps you are telling the truth. I have decided to take you to *el jefe* instead of killing you. I am a generous man. Luis may not be so generous, señors. If he thinks you are lying, he will have you shot."

"I suppose that's fair enough," Crow replied, feeling helpless without a gun. "We're here to negotiate a real simple business deal."

"Perhaps," the captain said carefully, continuing his study of Crow's face. "Return to your horses. My men have orders to shoot you if you try to escape. We ride to Hidalgo tonight."

"How about our guns?" Crow asked.

Cortez gave him a crooked grin. "You will not be needing them now, señor."

They rode at a walk through the darkness, surrounded by soldiers. One of Cortez's men took charge of the mule. At the rear of the procession, better than half of the men marched on foot through mountain passes and moonlit valleys. The captain rode at the front, glancing back now and then, occasionally talking to one of his lieutenants in a soft-spoken conversation Crow could not hear. Middleton and Hyde settled into a moody silence as soon as the ride was under way. Johnson rode alongside Crow, taking in every detail of the landscape without comment.

Several hours deeper into the mountains, the trail dropped sharply into a broad valley. Across the valley floor, tiny corn fields were arranged on both sides of the road. In late summer the stalks were sun-cured, turned white by relentless desert heat and days without rain. On the far side of the valley, at the base of a mountain, a pale adobe wall encircled a collection of huts and flat-roofed buildings. Near the heart of the pueblo, golden squares of lantern light beamed from a few windows. Now Crow remembered Hidalgo and the cattle-buying trip he made here ten years ago. The remoteness of the village struck him then as it did now, an unexpected oasis in the middle of barren, empty land.

"I reckon we're here," Johnson said quietly, looking up at the stars. "It's nigh unto midnight. Emptiest country I ever saw in my life. Hardly a soul between here an' the border."

"Silencio!" a nearby soldier snapped, drawing his pistol to aim it at Johnson's head, reining his horse closer.

Johnson merely shrugged and fell silent. The column started down a grade to the valley floor.

Crow's mind began to race. In the next hour, he would likely come face-to-face with Luis Zambrano again. He knew he would have to be careful, not allow his emotions to betray him when he set eyes on the bandit leader who had ordered the deaths of friends such as Harvey Bascome, Arturo Bustamante, Buck Davis, and Cotter Evans.

He had to be sure not to show any anger, no feeling at all. The most dangerous part of his plan was about to begin, and as best he could, he steeled himself for it. If Zambrano or anyone else recognized him from the bank robbery, he would be shot.

Crossing the valley, the whisper of dry cornshucks surrounded them when they passed the fields. Cortez's men moved silently toward the adobe wall, a silence broken only by the clatter of shod horses and the softer patter of sandals made by the foot soldiers marching at the rear. As they approached an opening in the wall, dogs began to bark, announcing their arrival. A moment later several armed guards came from the entrance to watch the procession enter Hidalgo, their rifles shouldered in a careless fashion. Somewhere in the village hungry goats bleated, and once, a burro brayed. Riding through the opening, Crow saw a plaza he remembered and the cantina where he drank *pulque* near the center of town. The cantina's windows were bright with lantern glow, and when he listened closely, he could hear someone strumming a guitar. As the horses plodded down a dirt road that would pass the plaza and the cantina, men came to the open windows to watch them ride in.

Crow's heart was beating faster. The moment he feared most was at hand. Would Zambrano, or one of the others, remember him from Carrizo Springs?

Cortez rode to the front of the cantina and swung down. Several of his men left their saddles. One of the soldiers guarding them drew his revolver and made a motion to dismount. More soldiers crowded around them before they reached the ground.

"*Alla,*" a soldier said, pointing to the cantina door with his gun barrel.

Single file, with Crow at the front, they walked through squares of light cast from the windows to reach an open doorway, escorted by half a dozen soldiers. Crow's mouth was suddenly dry as he walked past the door frame into the lamplit cantina.

Drinkers were seated at crude plank tables around the room. All eyes were on the door, and the guitar music stopped as soon as Crow and his men were ushered inside. The little cantina held roughly twenty hard-faced *pistoleros* and a few Mexican girls, but only one man commanded Crow's attention now.

In a corner, with his back to the wall, a bearded giant eyed the four newcomers, his elbows propped on a tabletop. A dusty sombrero rested on the back of a vacant hide-covered chair. Crow recognized Zambrano at once. For a time, the two men stared at each other. Seated beside the bandit leader, a pretty young girl with Indian features toyed with an empty glass.

"Quien es?" Zambrano asked, glancing at Captain Cortez briefly.

"Tejanos," Cortez replied. He aimed a thumb in Crow's direction. "This one says they have guns to sell. He wishes to speak with you, *Jefe.*"

Zambrano's cold black eyes moved up and down Crow's frame. *"Donde estas?* Where . . . these guns?"

"In Laredo," Crow answered, trying to remain calm. Did Zambrano recognize him? "We've got Winchester repeaters and crates of ammunition. Some Colt pistols, but I figure it's the rifles you need most."

Zambrano's heavy forehead knitted. "Why you come here?"

"We heard you were raising an army, and an army needs good rifles and plenty of cartridges. We decided to take a chance and ride down here to make you an offer. We can furnish you with new Winchesters at eighty dollars apiece, if you're interested."

For a moment Zambrano said nothing more, fixing Crow with an unwavering stare. Then he got up slowly and started around the table, spurs clanking heavily on the dirt floor, his face turned hard. When he stood in front of Crow, he was forced to gaze down to look him in the eye. Zambrano was well over six feet tall with a barrel chest and thick, muscular arms. His breath reeked of tequila when he spoke.

"The price is too high."

"It's a fair price," Crow replied, sensing real danger now, for it was easy to see Zambrano was angry. "It's against the laws of Texas to sell guns across the river. Me and my men are taking a big chance. If the Texas Rangers catch us before we get the rifles across, we'll go to jail. If the *federales* find us in Mexico with a wagon load of guns, we could lose everything, even our lives. Eighty dollars ain't much, considering the risks."

Zambrano's scowl deepened. "You ask too much," he growled as his right hand moved to the butt of his pistol.

"I reckon I'd listen to a reasonable offer," Crow said, determined not to show fear despite the unmistakable menace in the Mexican's voice. "If you agreed to take all the guns, I suppose we could take seventy-five."

"Mucho dinero," Zambrano said. "Maybeso I pay fifty-five."

"That ain't enough. Seventy-five is my best price."

A tense moment passed; then Crow saw Zambrano relax his gun hand. The silence grew heavier while Zambrano's gaze drifted to the other prisoners.

"Maybeso we talk," Zambrano said when his examination of the others ended. He turned to the Indian girl seated behind him. *"Más tequila. Un vaso. Andele!"*

The girl got up quickly and hurried away from the table to get a glass and a bottle of tequila. Zambrano pointed to a chair across the table; then he spoke to Captain Cortez, telling him to seat the others in another part of the room. The guards holstered their guns. Crow took a deep breath as he ambled over to the chair. For now, Zambrano was willing to discuss things.

The girl returned. She poured tequila into a clean glass, giving Crow sideways glances, and he was again taken with her dark beauty. *"Muchas gracias,"* he said, giving her a smile. She bowed politely and gave her long black hair a casual flip over her bare shoulders; then Zambrano dismissed her with a wave of his hand. She lifted the hem of her floor-length white skirt and headed for the bar.

Zambrano sat across from him, and quiet conversation resumed among the cantina patrons. "Tell me more about the guns," he said thickly as Crow took a sip of his drink.

"Brand new model '73s. Never been fired. Most are 38-40 caliber. Some will be 44-40s. I've got ammunition for both."

This information seemed to satisfy Zambrano. He shook his head and tasted his drink. "The price is too high."

"I'm the one taking all the chances. Selling guns to a revolutionary army in Mexico is dangerous business."

"But you are . . . how you say? A greedy man?"

"Maybe. I'm out to make a profit." Crow found that the girl was looking at him again, a fact that Zambrano did not fail to notice.

"You like Maria?" he asked. His thick beard parted in a grin.

"She's very pretty."

Zambrano motioned for the girl to come back to the table. "Is better you talk with her now. *En la mañana*, we agree on a price for the guns."

Crow watched the girl approach and felt old longings stir inside him. He could see the soft curves of her body inside her plain homespun dress. She sat gracefully in the chair beside him and smiled.

He was suddenly distracted by a movement across the table. Zambrano drew a long-barreled Colt .44 and aimed for the girl's head.

"The *puta* is yours tonight," he snarled, cocking his pistol. "She will help you make a better price for the guns."

Maria's hands started to tremble, and she quickly folded them in her lap, bowing her head with her eyes closed. Zambrano lowered his revolver, releasing the hammer gently with his thumb; then he chuckled softly and said, *"Mas tequila, mi hita."*

The girl picked up the bottle and poured, barely able to hold it without spilling tequila on the tabletop.

Chapter 15

The little hut was cool in the hours before dawn. Crow lay atop a cornshuck mattress below an open window, listening to the night sounds while the girl bathed him with a cloth dampened in a bucket of cool water. They had been shown to sleeping quarters: the others to a single adobe, Crow to the hut belonging to Maria. She dutifully removed his boots and clothes without uttering a word; then she began to bathe him by candlelight. He watched her, marveling at her deep chocolate eyes, her smooth oval face and shoulder-length hair. Zambrano had called her a whore, but Crow wondered if the threat at gunpoint was forcing her to do his bidding tonight. The girl seemed too young to be a *puta*.

A soft breeze fluttered curtains beside the window. The candle flickered. When her damp rag came to his genitals, he caught Maria's hand and held it.

"You don't have to do that," he whispered.

She lowered her eyes. *"El jefe* has ordered it," she said quietly.

"He won't have to know. I'll tell him you made me very happy tonight. It's the truth."

She smiled, revealing rows of even, white teeth. "You are kind, señor. My heart tells me you are a gentle man. This is a bad place for one like you. Luis will have you killed unless you agree to his price for the guns."

"Maybe. That's a chance I'll have to take." He released her hand. "Blow out the candle. It'll be daylight pretty soon, and we could both use some rest."

She got up and walked to the washstand with her water bucket. Before she snuffed out the flame, she turned her back to him and wriggled out of her skirt, revealing her naked hips, her slender waist. Then she removed her white blouse, and he caught a glimpse of one breast, a side view when she bent over to extinguish the candle. The room went dark. She returned to the bed and lay down beside him. A warm glow spread through his groin, yet he did not touch her, simply enjoying her presence next to him.

She stirred a moment later, moving against him, nestling her head on his shoulder. The warmth of her skin, the softness of her breasts touching his ribs, made it impossible to ignore her. He put one arm around her waist and turned slightly, facing her now.

"Tell me your name," she whispered, placing a dainty palm on his chest, the gentlest of touches.

"Jim Ed," he replied, his longing for the woman growing.

She repeated his name softly; then she raised her chin to kiss him lightly on the mouth. He returned the gentle pressure of her lips and tightened his embrace, for the moment forgetting about the danger he faced tomorrow, and in the days to come.

Holding the girl, he lost himself in pure pleasure. She lifted one slender brown leg and curled it around him. He could hear the whisper of her breathing and feel the soft caress of air against his cheek. By faint light from the stars beyond the window, he looked into her eyes, then watched her tiny nostrils flare. "You are very pretty," he told her, scenting her fragrance, a hint of soap from her hair.

She smiled and traced a fingertip along his cheek. He shivered despite the warmth of a summer night. Gooseflesh pimpled his skin, and he kissed her again, harder this time when almost-forgotten urges took control.

Outside the hut one of the guards lit a *cigarillo*, a dark reminder that when daybreak came he faced negotiations with Luis Zambrano over a wagon full of rifles. Zambrano meant to ply him with the charms of a young Indian girl to get what he wanted. For now, no one suspected the guns were a trap. Things could change suddenly, putting Crow's life in real danger. But for the time being, he pulled Maria closer to him and forgot about everything else.

Dawn brightened the window above the bed. He sat up slowly and shook his head to rid it of cobwebs. The girl lay beside him, curled into a ball. His gaze lingered on her naked body, the perfection of it, the swell of her ripe breasts, the subtle curve of her thighs, her tiny waist. Her long hair was spread over the bed linen like a fan, and he was stricken again by her raw, natural beauty.

He forced his thoughts to what lay ahead, a meeting with Zambrano to discuss price. The price for the guns was unimportant, and it was only necessary to appear to be concerned over the amount to be paid. All that really mattered was to lure Zambrano close to the border with the stolen money.

The plan could easily fail. If Zambrano sensed a trap, he would be too wary to ride into an ambush with the money. Fearing *federale* patrols, he might not agree to leave his mountain lair at all, calling for delivery of the rifles, which would doom the ambush attempt. There would be but one alternative: Crow and his men would have to rob Zambrano in order to get the money back, and that would mean a breakneck ride to reach the border if they were successful. Zambrano would hound them every step of the way. A single mistake, or a lame horse, would be a death sentence.

Looking out the window at the morning sky, Crow tried to strengthen his resolve by remembering the four dead citizens of Carrizo Springs, the penniless families there who couldn't make it without their money. Going after the stolen loot was the only choice he had. Despite the terrible risks, he owed it to the people who had counted on him to do everything he could in their behalf. He'd made it to the bandits' hideout and there was no turning back now.

Somewhere in the village, goats began to beg for food, and soon their cries became a chorus. The sky east of Hidalgo turned golden behind the jagged mountain peaks. He smelled smoke from early cooking fires carried on a warm breeze and got out of bed quietly without disturbing the girl's slumber. While he was dressing he listened for the guards outside the hut, wondering if they might have departed during the night. Or had they simply fallen asleep? It was important to find out how closely they were being watched. Last night, two men had accompa-

nied him to the hut, proof that Zambrano did not trust his
new visitors.

He crept to the thin plank door and opened it quietly.
A man slept against the adobe wall of the hut with his
sombrero covering his face. An old Spencer carbine
rested in his lap, and there was a pistol stuck in the
waistband of his pants. Beside him, an empty mescal
bottle resting on its side caught the first rays of sunlight
beaming from the mountaintops. The Mexican was snor-
ing softly into the crown of his hat.

Across the road another guard was slumped against the
wall of the hut where the others had been taken. Standing
back in the shadow of the doorway, Lee Johnson gave
Crow a silent nod as he, too, watched the sleeping guards.
A plentiful supply of mescal had kept the guards from
staying awake through the night. It could be an important
bit of information later on.

Hunger rumbled in Crow's stomach. He heard the
rustle of cornshucks behind him and turned to the bed.
Maria sat up, stretching and yawning. She smiled when
she saw Crow standing near the door.

"Buenas dias," she said sleepily, showing him every inch
of her nakedness when she got out of bed to don her dress.
She took a handful of water from the bucket and splashed
it on her face before she pulled on her blouse.

"Good morning," he said, recalling last night's inti-
macy with the girl. "You look even prettier in the morning."

She came over to him and stood on her tiptoes to kiss
his cheek, brushing her hair away from her face with a
careless motion of her hand. Her smile warmed him in a
way no other had for many lonely years. Fate had given

him no real chances to take a wife, and he had become accustomed to a solitary existence.

"I go. Fix food for you," she said.

"There's a guard outside," he told her.

Her smile widened. "It is only Santiago. He sleeps like *oso negro* . . . the black bear in winter."

He chuckled, still admiring the soft lines of her face and the deep color of her eyes. "A bear gets real mad if you wake him up."

"Not Santiago. He drinks too much of the mescal at night." She stepped around him and went out sound-lessly, merely glancing at the sleeping guard before she hurried down the road toward the cantina. He watched her walk away, recalling what it was like to hold her in his arms in the dark. Maria was easily the prettiest woman he'd ever known, and he knew he would always remem-ber the night he'd spent with her.

Johnson walked through the door of the adobe on the balls of his feet without disturbing the guard. He crossed the road and quietly entered Maria's hut. When the door was closed he spoke in a whisper.

"I slipped out last night to have a look around. Zam-brano sleeps in a big building near the stable. I counted four men who sleep in a front room of the place. They keep a couple of men posted outside. Makes six who stand betwixt us an' that money, if that's where they keep it. It makes sense they stash it close by in case there's trouble."

Crow was frowning. "We have to know for sure where the money is kept. If we decide to make a play for it and ride for the border, there's no room to make a mistake."

"I figure we've got plenty of time," Johnson said, cast-ing an eye out a window. "Long as they believe we've got guns to sell 'em, we can stall. But if we grab the money an' shoot our way out of here, we'll be in a hoss race plumb to the river. First thing we gotta do is get our guns back. The way Zambrano was actin' last night, that's liable to be a chore."

"It's natural enough for him to be suspicious of us right at first. Maybe the girl will help us . . ."

Johnson was grinning now. "She's one mighty pretty gal, that one is. Them two bounty hunters was complainin' how you got a woman all to yourself."

"She's hardly more than a girl, but I figure she knows where Zambrano hides the money. A small place like this, it'd be hard to keep it a secret."

"It could be a mistake to trust her," Johnson warned, his smile gone suddenly.

"I'll be careful."

Johnson crept to the door and peered outside; then he touched the brim of his hat in a lazy salute and walked softly back to the hut, glancing over his shoulder until he disappeared into the doorway across the road.

Crow went to the bucket and splashed water on his face, thinking about his next meeting with Zambrano. He rinsed out his mouth and thought about food. A few minutes later, Maria returned with a bundle of warm tortillas and a bowl of smoked goat meat and fried eggs. He took the bowl and ate hungrily. It had been days since they'd eaten anything but dry jerky.

The girl watched him eat while she was nibbling on a tortilla. She smiled every time he looked at her. He wondered if Johnson could be right, that it would be a mistake to trust her. She seemed too young and innocent to have dark motives, but she was certainly capable of betraying them out of fear. Last night, when Zambrano had held the gun to her head, her fear of him had appeared to be genuine enough.

When the bowl was empty she took it and left the hut. He walked to a window, examining the village in daylight. The wall around the pueblo was barely five feet high, probably designed to keep predators from the villagers' goats and sheep. But it also made the village a fortress, manned by soldiers who were properly armed. Hidalgo appeared to be a wise choice for someone who meant to raise a revolutionary army.

Leaning out the window, Crow looked down the road to the entrance they had ridden through last night. The adobe wall also made the village a prison for anyone kept inside under guard. If Crow and his men somehow got their hands on the money from Carrizo Springs, they would be forced to ride through the opening under heavy fire from the guards, further reducing their chances of making an escape.

The scrape of a boot near the door alerted him, and he drew his head back just in time. The guard Maria called Santiago peered inside, blinking sleepily.

"Bueno," he said when he saw Crow leaning against the wall. He was holding his pistol, aiming into the room. Satisfied, he turned away and closed the door behind him. A match was struck to a *cigarillo;* then all was quiet.

Crow sat on the edge of the mattress to await the meeting with Zambrano, noticing a tiny tremor in his hands. He'd been a good soldier once, albeit twenty years ago. It was a good thing back then to have a certain amount of fear before a battle, for it helped to keep him alive, keep him alert and watchful, never taking unnecessary chances. He was much older now, admittedly slower, perhaps more cautious.

Staring down at his hands, he wondered if a sense of duty would get him killed this time. Always before, he'd been given orders to follow. He was giving the orders now.

Chapter 16

Captain Cortez and four grim-faced soldiers came for him an hour before noon. The girl had not returned. Another guard had come to replace Santiago and the man watching the adobe where the others were being kept.

"*Vamos*," Cortez snapped. "*El jefe* wishes to see you now, Señor Smith. Come quickly. He does not like to be kept waiting."

Crow walked out into brilliant sunshine, pulling his hat brim over his face to shade his eyes. Surrounded by guards, he went with the captain and was surprised when they did not escort him back to the cantina. Instead, he was taken down a side street. At the end of the caliche lane, he saw a large adobe building beside a network of corrals.

I'm being taken to the place where they keep the money, he thought.

He was shown to the front door, where two bearded *pistoleros* rested on a wooden bench. One of them motioned Captain Cortez inside. Crow followed him, carefully taking in every detail of the place.

Four rawhide cots rested against the walls of an outer room. Cortez crossed to a dimly lit passageway, then to another large room where sunlight was kept from the windows by heavy cloth curtains. Seated at a table in the middle of the room, Luis Zambrano watched Crow approach through hooded eyelids. Crow was halfway to the table before he noticed Maria in a dark corner.

The girl was bound to a chair with her arms behind her. A cloth was tied over her mouth. Even in the poor light Crow could see the bruises on her face and a swelling below her right eye. A tiny trickle of blood ran from her lips, spotting her soft white blouse and the creamy skin above her breasts.

"Why have you done this to the girl?" he demanded, halting a few feet from the table.

Zambrano smiled wickedly. "She no speak truth. She say you tell her nothing about where you keep the guns."

"I already told you that they're close to Laredo. Some of my men are watching them, to keep the Texas Rangers from finding the wagon. There's no reason to hurt the woman. She knows nothing. I didn't tell her anything at all."

Zambrano turned his gaze to Maria. He grunted and shook his head. *"Puta!"* he spat angrily; then he looked at Crow again.

For a moment they merely stared at each other. Zambrano seemed to be considering something.

"I pay sixty *norteamericano* dollars for the rifles," he finally said, scratching through his beard with a thick-fingered hand. "Is a very generous offer . . ."

"Not enough," Crow replied, sounding firm about it. "I'd listen to an offer of seventy-five."

"Is too much," Zambrano snarled. He slammed a

meaty fist on the tabletop and held up six fingers. "Sixty *dólares!* You must also bring them here to me!"

"It's out of the question. Me and my men will take them across the river at some safe place, but we won't bring them to Hidalgo. It's too dangerous. We don't know anything about this part of the country . . ."

At that, Zambrano came slowly to his feet and drew his gun. He aimed across the table. "Then tell me, señor, how you find this place. Do not take me for *una idiota!*"

Staring into the muzzle of the pistol, Crow said, "We asked around in Nuevo Laredo. Somebody told us to come to Hidalgo to look for you. It's that simple." Sensing a hint of doubt in Zambrano's eyes, he continued, "And I won't do business with any man who sticks a gun in my face. If you don't want the Winchesters at seventy-five, me and my men will be on our way back to Texas."

The gun did not waver. "You tell *los federales* where we are hiding. They will attack us."

Crow shrugged. "No reason to do that. I'd be taking a big chance myself. They'd want to know what we were doing down here in the first place. They could arrest us on suspicion of gun running to a revolutionary army. I'd have to be crazy to talk to them."

Zambrano hesitated, giving Crow the once-over. "Seventy-five is too much." He lowered his pistol and placed it on the table in front of him. "Sit. We will talk more. I send Ramon to bring us food and tequila."

A tense moment had passed. Crow nodded once, relieved when the Colt was no longer aimed at his chest. "Let the girl go. She has done nothing wrong. I'd be obliged if you sent some food to my men. Then we'll talk about the price. I came down here to do business with you. If we can strike a bargain, I can sell you more guns later on. The deal can be good for both of us."

Zambrano glanced to the doorway behind Crow. "*Comida para los Tejanos,*" he said, then he walked over to Maria and drew a knife from his belt. He cut her bindings and took the gag from her mouth. "*Vamos,*" he told her quietly.

The girl stood up and hurried from the room without looking at Crow, holding one hand over her bleeding mouth. When the sound of her footsteps faded, Zambrano pointed to a vacant chair at the far end of the table. "*Sientate,*" he said, lowering himself into his seat, paying no heed to the gun before him now.

Crow sat down, feeling relief he dared not show. At least the negotiations would resume without bloodshed. "I might consider an offer of seventy dollars for those rifles if we can agree on how and where they'll be delivered. I know this place above Laredo where the river is shallow. Nobody goes there. I could cross them there after dark, maybe drive down a mile or two to a meeting place we agreed on. But I'd have to see the color of your money first, so I know you can pay."

"You do not trust me?" Zambrano asked, feigning surprise.

"It's just good business. It ain't personal."

A wry grin passed briefly across Zambrano's face. "You are a careful *hombre,* señor. It is as you say, good business to see the color of money." He glanced toward another corner of the room and then pushed himself up with the help of the table.

At first, Crow was puzzled by the Mexican's behavior, until Zambrano removed a few blankets from a pile against the back wall. Only then did he see the canvas bags stacked in the corner, and the inscription, "Dimmit County Bank," on each of them.

Zambrano picked up one bag and brought it to the table, where he dumped out the contents in front of Crow. Neat bundles of currency lay in a pile before him.

"American dollars," he said, hiding his excitement the best he could. "But it don't look like enough to buy two hundred new rifles and crates of ammunition."

"There is more," Zambrano said, looking to the corner.

Crow made a show of examining the other bags; then he shook his head. "Looks like we can make a deal. You'll need fourteen thousand dollars for the Winchesters. Another three thousand or so for the cartridges. There are some Colt pistols and a few shotguns in the load. I'll throw them in for a total price of eighteen thousand dollars, including the wagon and a team of mules."

"Is too much," Zambrano snarled, pointing to the money on the tabletop. "I pay only fifteen thousand."

Crow wagged his head side to side. "It ain't enough. I'd lose money."

"You are a hard man, Señor Smith. The price is too high. I pay fifteen. *No mas!*"

"Then I don't reckon we can do any business," Crow said as he started to get to his feet. Zambrano would mistrust him if he gave in too easily. "If you'll ask your captain to give us back our horses, we'll be on our way."

Zambrano watched him rise from the chair, and Crow was almost certain he saw disbelief on the Mexican's face. Had Zambrano merely been baiting him? Was this some kind of test?

Footsteps from the adjoining room announced the return of the *pistolero* named Ramon, carrying a bottle of tequila and a platter laden with roasted chicken, potatoes, and ears of corn.

"Ah, now we eat," Zambrano said. "Sit. We talk more after we are full."

Delicious smells filled Crow's nostrils. Despite an ample breakfast, his mouth watered. "Not much left to talk about," he said doubtfully, eyeing the platter piled high with food as Ramon put it on the table before them. A plump Mexican woman followed the *pistolero*, carrying a cloth bundle of tortillas and a bowl of spicy salsa. Bits of green cilantro floated in the sauce.

"Sit," Zambrano said again. "Is our custom in Mexico to eat before we do business." He glanced down to the gun on the tabletop briefly. "If we no can agree, I will maybeso let you and your *compadres* go back to Texas." He gave Crow a one-sided grin. "Maybeso I kill you, so you no tell *los federales* where we are hiding."

Ramon and the woman left the room, leaving Crow standing before Zambrano alone. In a corner were bags of money belonging to the citizens of Carrizo Springs. Bundles of currency littered the table. Zambrano's pistol lay between them. In a contest to see who could reach the gun first, Crow stood a chance of winning. But then he would be surrounded by armed men, perhaps a hundred or more, facing the impossible task of shooting his way out of a walled village with the money. Making a grab for the gun would be a fool's move, and he let that notion drop. "I already told you why we can't run the risk of talking to the *federales*, and you know I'm telling the truth. We're just as interested in avoiding them as you are. We ain't looking to spend the rest of our lives in a Mexican jail. We'd have nothing to gain by telling them where to find you. Besides that, if the pay was right, me and my men might do a little fighting for your side if we can do business on this load of rifles. We're all experienced soldiers."

For the moment Zambrano ignored the food, appraising Crow carefully. "*El negro*," he said thoughtfully. "Capitan Cortez say the black one is a good shot. Maybeso I no kill you now. Sit. We talk."

"I never did like being threatened. We came down here on business. There won't be many places where you can buy repeating rifles. I'm offering you the chance to arm your men with the best guns money can buy. Looks like you'd show more gratitude."

"*Posiblemente* I have been wrong, Señor Smith. When *mi capitan* bring you here, I no trust you. Sit. Eat. We talk."

Evidencing what he hoped would be just enough reluctance to be convincing, Crow sat back down. Zambrano was no longer watching him, but pulling a chicken leg from the platter to take a generous bite. Crow took an ear of corn and nibbled one end, wondering if he'd put Zambrano's worries to rest.

"How many men you have with the guns?" Zambrano asked.

The question caught him off guard. Counting Tinker, Pedro Garza and his cousin, he could only think of three who might help with the ambush. "Just three. We've got them well hidden, but a man can never be too careful."

Around a mouthful of chicken, Zambrano smiled. "I, too, am being careful, Señor Smith. If you tell me *la verdad,* the truth about the guns, we do business, you and me."

"I've got no reason to double-cross you. You pay me a fair price and we'll meet just south of the river."

Zambrano grunted, stuffing a tortilla into his cheek; then he uncorked the tequila and poured into two badly smudged glasses. "Tell me, señor, did you like the woman?"

"She's very pretty. A bit on the young side."

Smacking his lips, Zambrano nodded. *"Bueno.* She is yours, for I am a generous man. There is only the price for the guns to be settled."

Crow took a piece of chicken. "It must be a fair price. I'm real grateful for the girl last night, but I don't figure I'll be needing her now. She'd only be in the way while we're trying to get that wagon across the river, and it's one hell of a long ride through those mountains to get back home."

"Then she is yours until you leave Hidalgo. You, and your three *compadres*, will be free to go where you wish in the pueblo now. This night, *en la noche*, we drink at the cantina. *En la mañana*, you may go. I offer each of you one hundred dollars to fight with us on the side of *la revolución*. A hundred more on the first day of each month. I will pay sixteen thousand dollars for the guns and cartridges. As you can see, I am a very generous man."

Crow knew it was best not to sound too eager to accept the proposition. Best of all, they would be given their freedom to roam around the village tonight. Something was making Zambrano less cautious . . . perhaps now he was beginning to trust them. "I still don't like the price, but I suppose I can live with it. I can have the rifles a mile below the old Las Minas crossing in four days, if you happen to know the place."

Zambrano leaned forward in his chair, still chewing bites of meat. "I know every inch of the border, Señor Smith," he said in a hoarse voice containing the suggestion of a threat. "My men and I will wait for you at Las Minas with the money. If you do not bring the guns in four days, or if you try to trick me, I swear before *Dios* I will kill you."

There was something about the look on Zambrano's face that sent a tiny shiver down Crow's spine, perhaps something in his voice. "We'll be there. Let's drink a toast to our agreement. I'll tell my men about the hundred dollars a month you're offering mercenaries, too. I figure they'll want to sign on with your army, and the same goes for me. With repeating rifles, you stand a good chance against the *federales*. And I can promise you that there are more guns where these came from, if you can raise the money."

They lifted glasses in a toast. Crow hoped the slight tremor in his hand didn't show.

Chapter 17

When the guard was ordered away from the hut by Captain Cortez, Crow lowered his voice and spoke to the others as the soldiers were walking toward the cantina. "Zambrano has given us our freedom to move around in the village. I think I've got him convinced we're shooting straight about the rifles. I saw the place where he keeps the money. Now we've got to decide if there's a chance we can rob him tonight and make a run for the border. Or do we wait and try to ambush him when he comes north to buy the guns."

"Robbin' them inside this wall is gonna be mighty goddamn risky," Middleton said. "Gettin' our horses through that gate without gettin' them shot out from under us will be tough, an' we'll be dodgin' a hell of a lot of lead ourselves."

"It'll be dangerous," Johnson agreed, casting a look out one of the windows, "but jus' maybe there's another way out of this place. This mornin' I saw a herd of goats movin' up that mountain yonder. Never did see 'em pass by on the way to that opening in the wall where we come in the day before. Maybe there's another hole in the wall someplace, a gate we can't see from here."

"It'll pay to look," Crow said, thinking out loud. "One of us needs to find out where they're keeping our horses. I saw the stable a while ago, right behind the big building where Zambrano keeps the money. It figures to be the only place where they can stable our horses. I saw fifty or sixty horses in those pens, but no sign of ours."

"What about our guns?" Hyde asked softly, watching the doorway.

"No way to tell where they are right now," Crow answered. "Finding our horses and another way out of this place is the first thing we have to do. If there's another opening in the wall, a gate on the back side of the village, it could be our ticket out of here with the money. One of us has to look for another hole in that wall."

"I'll go," Johnson said. "I'll amble around for an hour or so whilst somebody else looks for the horses."

"This is plumb crazy," Middleton said. "There's too many of 'em for us to shoot our way out of here. You know damn good'n well they'll have plenty of guards around that money tonight, an' we ain't even got our guns."

Crow let out a sigh. "All we're doing right now is checking into a few things. Zambrano agreed to meet us below the border at Las Minas to buy the rifles. If we can't figure a way to rob that room where they keep the money, we'll clear out and set up an ambush near Las Minas. I'll round up some men from Carrizo Springs who can shoot . . ."

Johnson went to the door and peered around the frame while Middleton and Hyde were exchanging doubtful looks.

"If there's another hole in this here wall," Johnson said, squinting into the sun's glare, "maybe that's what we oughta try an' do . . . rob them an' make a run for it. Like I said, it'll be a hoss race if we get the money an' take off for the river. Ain't gonna be easy, either way. The tough part is gonna be gettin' our hosses, and us, outside the wall in one piece."

"Bullshit!" Middleton snapped, glaring at Johnson. "The hard part is robbin' that room without any guns. You figurin' they'll just hand over the money if we ask real nice?"

"Hold on," Crow said, coming between them. "For now all we're doing is looking things over."

Middleton turned and stalked over to the door. "This whole idea is downright stupid. Me an' Roy are headed down to that cantina for a drink or two. There's a hundred armed men in this lousy little town, an' every one of them will be shootin' at us if we try to rob that room. Until you come up with a better idea, you can count us out of it."

The pair went out, leaving Crow alone with Johnson. For a time, neither man spoke.

"Take a look at the wall," Crow said. "See if there is another way out. I'll check on the horses. Remember, they'll be watching us."

Johnson nodded and stepped out, strolling casually to the south as though he wasn't looking for anything in particular. Crow started back toward the corrals by a route that would take him past the adobe building. A blistering afternoon sun shone down on Hidalgo. Most of the villagers, and the soldiers, were inside to escape the heat. Here and there, dark-skinned children played in the shadows between the huts and small shops.

When he passed the building, he noted two more *pistoleros* guarding the entrance, slumped on a bench beneath a porch fashioned from thatched mesquite limbs. The guards watched him amble by without showing any particular interest.

He came to a row of pole corrals where fifty or sixty horses and mules were kept. At the back of the last corral he spotted Dixie and Johnson's red roan. His gray stood hipshot, swishing flies with its tail. He found the bounty hunters' horses in the same pen. All in all, the Mexicans had a poor collection of horseflesh, most of them looking rawboned, half-starved.

We can win a horse race, he thought, if we can get out of here without any bullet holes.

On a top rail of the corral, dozens of saddles rested with bridles hung from the saddle horns. He easily located his own rig and the others, since most of the saddles were of the Mexican variety. It appeared that no one was guarding the horses, although the guards posted in front of the adobe could see the pens from a distance. Behind the corrals, the adobe wall ran east and west with no visible opening Crow could find. They were trapped inside with only one way out, unless Johnson found something in another part of the village.

He turned away from the fence and started back, glancing at the adobe now and then as he trudged past. The guards were watching him from the porch, and he was sure they would report his movements to Zambrano. It seemed natural enough for anyone to inspect the condition of his mounts before making a long ride through dry mountains.

When he reached the central plaza there were dozens of men gathered in small clusters where live oaks provided shade. A well occupied the center of the plaza. Most of the men were of the type Captain Cortez commanded, local farmers and goat herders who stayed apart from the hardened *pistoleros*. Zambrano's army was a mixture of *peons* and bandits. Crow knew the *pistoleros* were the men to fear if he and his men tried to escape from Hidalgo with the money sacks.

He was wondering about Maria as he walked to the cantina, when a cry went up near the gate. Men carrying rifles rushed to the opening, some pointing to a spiraling cloud of dust in the distance. Looking below the dust, Crow saw a lone horseman riding toward Hidalgo at a full gallop. Someone was bringing news to the village, news requiring great haste.

The rider reached the opening in the wall and jerked his lathered horse to a bounding halt. More soldiers hurried over to hear what was being said by the messenger. Shouted voices arose from the throng around the horseman. Men were pointing to the east.

A soldier trotted away from the group, rounding the corner that would take him to Zambrano's headquarters. Crow watched the affair awhile longer, puzzling over the excitement. Middleton and Hyde came to the door of the cantina to see what the ruckus was about.

Captain Cortez appeared from a doorway into one of the huts with a young Mexican girl at his side. A soldier ran over to him and said something, pointing east.

Middleton saw Crow at the edge of the plaza and started across the road. "What the hell is goin' on?" he asked.

"Can't say for sure, but it looks like somebody's bringing bad news."

Cortez shouted an order, and all at once, men were

running for the corrals. At the same time, Zambrano emerged from his adobe flanked by half a dozen *pistoleros*. Soldiers idling away time in the plaza were moving in every direction now. The sleepy little village became a beehive of activity. Then someone in the crowd cried, *"Los federales!"*

Zambrano and his gunmen hurried to the opening in the wall where the messenger was relating what he had seen.

"Mexican army must be close," Middleton said. "Otherwise, they wouldn't be so excited."

"I hope Zambrano doesn't blame it on us," Crow replied. "If he thinks we led them here, he'll have us shot . . ."

Zambrano wheeled around as though he was looking for something. When he saw Crow and Middleton, he pointed to them and said something to his *pistoleros*. Faces turned, and when they did Crow felt a sinking sensation in the pit of his stomach.

"He believes we brought them here," Crow whispered. "This could be real trouble."

Some of the *pistoleros* drew their guns when they started toward the plaza. It was quickly evident they meant to corral the men from Texas. Without weapons, Crow felt completely helpless now, and he wondered if Zambrano had ordered executions for the four of them.

"Sweet Jesus," Middleton exclaimed breathlessly, looking over his shoulder for a way to escape. "They're gonna kill us sure as hell . . ."

"Stand your ground," Crow said under his breath. "Won't do any good to run. We'll have to convince him we didn't have anything to do with this."

Four *pistoleros* came up to Crow and Middleton. A fifth

went to the cantina door, motioning for Hyde to come outside using the barrel of his gun. Pistols were trained on them as Zambrano walked stiffly toward the group. Meanwhile, soldiers scurried back and forth, moving in the direction of the corrals.

When Zambrano arrived he pointed a finger to the east with an angry set to his bearded jaw. *"Federales* are in the mountains," he said, piercing Crow with a look.

Crow shrugged. "We'd be fools to bring them here. If they find us with a revolutionary army, they'll know what we're up to. We'll be shot on sight, or tossed in jail."

For a moment Zambrano appeared to be considering what Crow said, glancing now and then at the mountains to the east.

"How many of them are coming?" Crow asked, seizing a quick opportunity to buy time. "If you'll give us back our guns and pay us the hundred dollars you offered, we'll help you fight them off. That oughta prove we didn't lead them here . . ."

Zambrano's gaze returned to Crow, and there was a hard, questioning look in his eyes. Near the horse pens, mounted men had begun to assemble.

"Antonio say they are like ants," Zambrano replied. "We have been betrayed to Comandante Obregon! We must attack them first, before they surround Hidalgo! They come too soon, before we can buy the guns we need! Some of us must attack them now, while others move our supplies and ammunition deeper into the mountains."

"We'll fight," Crow said again, "so long as we get paid for it. But it's a better idea to send us north as fast as we can ride, so we can make the deal to sell you those Winchesters."

"Sí, the guns. If only we had them now . . ." He

frowned as a platoon of foot soldiers was forming in the plaza. "I will send Capitan Cortez to attack Obregon. You and your *compadres* will help us protect the supplies until we are safe in the mountains to the west. Then you go to Laredo and bring the weapon to Las Minas. We must have the rifles to fight Obregon." It was then he noticed Johnson's absence. "Where is *el negro?*"

The question required Crow to think fast. He gave a weak grin. "Looking for a girl, I reckon. He took a fancy to little Maria and said he wanted to find a woman like that for himself."

There was doubt on Zambrano's face. "Find him. Come to the corrals. Ramon will give you your guns. Saddle your horses. We leave *muy pronto.*" He spoke to Ramon in rapid Spanish, and at the same time, the *pistoleros* holstered their guns.

Crow motioned Middleton and Hyde away to find their horses. In the mass confusion in the streets, he wondered how difficult it would be to find Lee Johnson. Zambrano was suspicious of Johnson's absence. Hurrying down the road past the column of mounted soldiers, he scanned the huts and side streets, hoping to find the fourth member of his party before someone spotted Johnson prowling around the adobe wall.

"What are we gonna do?" Middleton asked, matching Crow stride for stride toward the horse pens.

"We wait. Maybe the right opportunity will come along after these soldiers pull out. Kinda depends on how many men are staying behind to move the ammunition . . . and the money."

"He said he'd give us back our guns," Middleton whispered. "It'll sure as hell change things if he does."

"Damn right it will," Hyde said, having overheard the

quiet remark. "Wish the hell that damn darkie would get his ass back here. We're gonna need every gun we've got if we aim to pull this off."

At the end of the column of horsemen, standing in the shadow of an adobe hut across from the corrals, Crow saw Johnson beckoning to them. The hut had long been abandoned, its walls crumbling to ruin, the roof fallen in. Johnson seemed to be trying to remain hidden behind one wall. "Yonder's Lee," he said quietly, "and it looks like he don't want anyone to see him. I sure hope there ain't some kind of trouble."

"Maybe he found another way out of this place," Middleton said as they cut off the road to come around the back side of the empty hut.

"Stay here," Crow told them. "I'll find out what he wants without attracting too much attention."

He rounded a corner of the hut. At a spot where a wall had fallen to rubble, Johnson motioned him inside. Before Crow could form a question, he glanced down where Johnson was pointing and immediately froze in his tracks. The body of a *pistolero* lay in a pool of blood.

"What happened?" Crow asked thickly, feeling his heart begin to pound.

"I had to kill him with my knife. Lucky they didn't find my Bowie when they searched us." Johnson reached into a pocket of his pants. Lying in his palm was Crow's Dimmit County sheriff's badge. "He was goin' through our saddlebags. Found this. I saw him jus' in time. Wasn't no choice but to kill him an' drag him in here. Nobody saw it, on account of all the excitement. I heard 'em say the *federales* are comin'."

Crow's thoughts were racing. "Somebody'll miss him before too long. Means we haven't got much time. Zambrano agreed to give us back our horses and guns, but this changes everything as soon as they find the body. Let's hope they don't discover him until we get saddled and get our guns back."

Johnson peered around the break in the wall. For now, no one came close to the abandoned hut. "I found a gate at the back of the village," he said. "Made from heavy timber. It's real small, but we can squeeze through. It's where they take the goat herds in and out."

Crow knew the information could prove to be very useful if things went awry. "Let's get saddled," he said softly, after a final look at the corpse, "and pray for a little bit of luck."

Chapter 18

The column of cavalry was moving, forty men riding in pairs behind Captain Cortez. Near the plaza, foot soldiers marched to the front gate shouldering ancient single-shot rifles and belts full of cartridges. Crow watched them as he cinched his saddle on Dixie, hoping no one would notice the body in the crumbling adobe. Judging by the number of horses remaining in the corrals, Zambrano was keeping less than twenty men in Hidalgo to ferry the ammunition and supplies into the mountains. Quite suddenly the odds were better. The stolen money would be guarded by fewer men; the chances improved that it could be taken without having to escape the gunfire from more than a hundred rifles and pistols.

I should have remembered that badge, he thought, tying off the latigo strap absently. A careless mistake had almost cost him his life.

Ramon emerged from the big adobe carrying their guns, the Winchesters and gun belts, and the bounty hunters' shotguns. Crow left his gray to meet Ramon on the road before he came in sight of the hut where the corpse was hidden.

"Gracias," he said, taking the weapons one at a time, the Remington rolling block rifle belonging to Johnson after he took the pistols and rifles. Hyde and Middleton came over to strap on their gun belts and take rifles and shot-guns. A *pistolero* led three mules to the front of the building bearing pack saddles. Moments later a thick-bodied Mexican came outside with a crate of ammunition to begin filling the packs. As Crow was buckling on his gun belt, more of Zambrano's men came from the building bearing wooden crates to tie them aboard the mules. Crow took a rough count of the men he could see. Nine *pistoleros* helped with the loading. Four more were at the corrals saddling horses. Including Ramon and Zambrano himself, fifteen men had stayed behind. He wondered how long it would be before someone missed the dead man. Would they conduct a search for him?

Looking east beyond the wall, he could see Captain Cortez's columns moving across the valley. Soon they would be out of hearing distance if shots were fired. Although they were moving slowly to keep pace with the foot soldiers, in another quarter hour they would be out of sight behind the mountains.

He walked to the corral fence where Johnson was sad-dling his roan, handing him his gun belt and rifle. "Make sure they're both loaded," he said, keeping his voice low. "Our chance may come any minute now. It'll be up to you to lead us to that back gate if there's any shooting. They've still got guards posted at the front."

Johnson nodded and strapped on his pistol. Hidden between two horses, Middleton and Hyde checked the loads in their guns.

"We'd be better off to wait until Cap'n Cortez is out of sight," Johnson said, chambering a cartridge into his rifle.

"Hope it works out that way," Crow replied, "but we'll have to take our chance whenever it comes."

A *pistolero* led Zambrano's big black horse away from the corrals. A silver-studded saddle was cinched to its back. The animal was the best conditioned among the Mexicans' horses, its sleek black coat shining from many brushings.

"I figure we can win a horse race," Crow added quietly, "if we can get clear of this wall to get a good lead on them. I reckon it all depends on getting the right breaks." He looked east again. Cortez's columns were headed toward a high pass between two rocky peaks now. "A little bit longer," he whispered to himself, judging the distance. Cortez would still hear the crackle of gunfire.

Ramon and another *pistolero* led a pair of rangy sorrels from the pens to the front of the adobe. Ramon went inside. Crow pretended to busy himself with his saddle cinch, standing behind the gray to attract less attention. Half a minute later Ramon and Zambrano emerged from the doorway carrying four canvas bags from the Dimmit County Bank. A third gunman followed with two more money sacks. The bags were secured to Zambrano's black and the two sorrels as the last crates of cartridges were being tied to the mules. Zambrano turned now and then to watch the columns climb toward the high pass. He carried his sawed-off shotgun on a strap hanging from his left shoulder. Crow remembered what the wicked little gun had done to Harvey Bascome's head.

Johnson edged up beside Crow, holding his Remington beside his leg. "If we was to cut down on 'em soon as they got mounted, we'd catch 'em by surprise. They won't be expectin' it."

Crow felt a tightness in his chest, thinking about the

risk. As soon as the shooting started the air would be full of flying lead. His palms started to sweat while gripping the rifle hidden behind his horse. At a distance of less than a hundred yards the gunfire would be deadly. "I'll tell Bill and Roy to be ready," he whispered. "Looks like this is about the best chance we'll have to catch Zambrano off guard."

Moving slowly, he lowered the Winchester and walked around the gray's rump to reach the bounty hunters. "Get ready," he said quietly. "Soon as they're all mounted we'll start shooting. Make damn sure of your aim. Their horses will scatter in every direction when we empty those saddles. Remember the reason we came here. Those six money sacks are what we're after."

Hyde was frowning a little. "It's liable to be a job gettin' to the money unless we can kill 'em all right away, but you can count on us. We'll get our share."

Crow left them standing behind their horses. Zambrano and his men were occupied with securing the money bags, thus no one seemed to notice when Crow returned to his horse. One by one, a few of the *pistoleros* climbed into their saddles. Crow counted five, then six, then two more. Zambrano and Ramon remained on the ground, inspecting the final loading of each mule. It appeared that Crow and his men were momentarily forgotten in the haste to pull out of Hidalgo.

A distant sound came from the far side of the valley, the faint rattle of gunshots. Crow wheeled around for a view of the pass. Cortez and his cavalry had ridden out of sight. The last foot soldiers were breaking ranks, scattering in every direction amid the steady crackle of gunfire.

"*Los federales!*" someone in the village shouted.

"*Andele! Vamanos!*" a mounted *pistolero* cried.

Zambrano's head was turned toward the battle sounds. He made a fist and shook it in the air. *"Bastardos!"*

Three more *pistoleros* hurried into their saddles, when an unexpected explosion thundered from Crow's left, the roar of a Winchester carbine. Hyde's rifle was aimed at a Mexican gunman aboard a goose-hipped bay. The slug lifted the *pistolero* out of his saddle and sent him spinning toward the ground.

"No!" Crow shouted, knowing the warning came too late. Hyde had fired minutes too soon.

Middleton fired as horses plunged away from the front of the adobe to escape the sudden noise. A rider toppled, spilling his sombrero, arms windmilling helplessly before he fell in a heap near the doorway. Hyde fired again; then a gunshot rang out from Johnson's big Remington before Crow could bring his rifle to his shoulder.

Zambrano's black gelding bolted away, trailing loose reins, twin money bags fastened to the silver-plated saddle. Zambrano made a dive for the reins as he was clawing his pistol from its holster, but the horse lunged too quickly. It bounded for the corrals, whickering, mane and tail flying in the air. Zambrano fell on his stomach, bringing his pistol to bear on the four riderless horses where Crow and his men took cover. The Colt spat flame, and there was a popping noise; then Hyde's sorrel reared, squealing with pain when a bullet struck its shoulder.

Crow aimed and fired at a fast-moving target, a *pistolero* bending low over his horse's neck. The Winchester slammed into his shoulder amid a deafening roar. The Mexican was torn from his saddle, driven into the adobe wall by the force of a speeding slug at close range. He fell, arms and legs askew at the base of the wall, shrouded by a filmy dust cloud.

"Son of a bitch!" Hyde shouted as his horse collapsed on the ground in front of him, hooves thrashing, churning up dust.

Crow levered another shell into the firing chamber as Dixie fidgeted, bunching powerful muscles, frightened by the noise when Crow used the gun. A staccato of pistol shots came from the front of the adobe. Molten lead whined through the air high and wide, missing hastily taken targets.

Middleton triggered off a shot. Somewhere in the dust and confusion, a man screamed. Loose horses galloped away from the fight. A pack mule bolted from the front of the building, snorting, its long ears pinned flat against its neck.

Crow fired at a fleeting shape in the dust cloud, the dim outline of a man aboard a racing horse. He missed badly, for now his gray gelding fought the pull of tied reins, blocking his vision when it pulled back.

Johnson's heavy rifle thundered. A man on foot tumbled to the ground beside a window of the building, sprawling on his face while Crow ejected the spent shell from his Winchester as quickly as he could. Dixie snorted, churning the ground with nervous hooves before Crow's rifle was ready to fire again. A brief pause in the shooting allowed some of the dust to settle; then the roar of guns resumed in earnest. One of the sorrels bearing money bags galloped toward Crow, showing the whites of its eyes, flicking its ears back and forth. A deep gash across its rump dribbled blood on the caliche road. Crow jumped in front of the terrified animal and caught its reins. In the same instant, a gun banged from the door of the adobe, sending a ball of white-hot lead through the crown of Crow's hat.

"Whoa there!" he cried, attempting to halt the flight of the racing horse by pulling on its reins. He threw his rifle down and made a grab for the canvas bags looped from the saddle horn. The bullet piercing his hat had been mere inches too high to split open his skull, and now his heart was beating rapidly. He seized the drawstrings on the money bags and jerked the sacks free just as a gun sounded. Something struck the sorrel gelding's rear leg, and it plummeted to the ground on its chest, bawling in pain.

From the corner of his eye he saw Johnson running through the swirling dust, chasing Zambrano's black horse and the bags of money bouncing against its withers. Crow dropped the sacks he'd taken from the sorrel, intending to go after the black himself, when suddenly a terrific explosion drowned out the other guns. Crow wheeled toward the sound, crouching. Ramon stood at the entrance of the adobe building with a long-barreled rifle to his shoulder. Roy Hyde staggered backward with his hands pressed to his belly, emitting a cry that reminded Crow of a wounded cougar. A tiny fountain of crimson spewed from the back of his shirt. His knees buckled. He went down, landing on the seat of his pants, bellowing at the top of his lungs, his face twisted in agony. Blood squirted from the hole in his shirt, turning the ground around him a muddy brown color. He turned his head to look at his partner. Tears streamed from his eyes. "I'm shot, Bill!" he screamed, looking down at his blood-reddened hands.

Another gunshot blasted from the doorway. Hyde's expression seemed to change instantly. His hat flew off, fluttering like a wounded bird in flight while bone and flesh erupted from the back of his skull. Bone fragments and pulpy bits of skin and hair fell to the roadway behind him. He toppled over backward in a pool of blood, his right boot twitching with death throes.

Twenty yards away, Johnson seized the money sacks from the black's withers and raced for the corral fence. Two more bags of money were missing, tied to the back of a sorrel galloping off into the village. Crow picked up his rifle. "Let's clear out!" he shouted as a renewed burst of gunfire came from the windows and door of the adobe.

Johnson swung aboard his roan, leaning over the horse's neck to make as small a target as possible, hanging the canvas bags from his saddle horn. Crow grabbed the pair of money sacks near his feet and made a dive for the seat of his saddle as bullets whistled overhead, barely able to breathe in the heat of the exchange of gunshots. Middleton jumped to his horse's back and drummed his heels into its ribs, sending the gelding into a powerful lunge away from the corral fence.

The three of them were off in a breakneck gallop toward the south side of the village with guns cracking behind them. Lead whispered through the air, the eerie sing-song of speeding bullets. Slugs plowed little furrows all around their horses' pounding hooves, kicking up tiny spits of caliche dust on either side of their escape route. Bending low in the saddle, Crow heeled the gray to full speed, praying for a miracle, that no bullet would find him or his horse before they made the gate on the south side of town.

Johnson's roan swerved suddenly to the right. A riderless sorrel horse galloped between the adobe huts, its mane and tail flying. Crow saw bags from the Dimmit County Bank flopping against the horse's shoulders, and he understood Johnson's quick change of direction. Rein-

ing Dixie, he drummed his heels into the gelding's sides
to give chase. The last of the money was only fifty yards
away. Despite the hail of bullets screaming around them,
he knew he had to make one last desperate try at getting
his hands on it before they left the village.

Johnson's roan caught up to the sorrel. He leaned out
of the saddle and grabbed the sacks with his horse running
full stride. The drumming of hooves seemed louder now
as the horses galloped between the huts. Dixie outpaced
Middleton's gelding by a length, then two, until at last the
riders neared the adobe wall where it encircled the goat
pens.

Johnson stood in his stirrups, pointing to a spot behind
the fences where the goats were kept at night. The sound
of gunshots was farther away when he cried, "Yonder's
the gate!"

Crow saw a tiny opening in the wall, blocked by a gate
fashioned from weathered planking. Pounding his heels
into his horse's ribs, he rode for the gate while glancing
over his shoulder. Dust curled from the roadway behind
them. Below the dust, mounted *pistoleros* charged in headlong pursuit, guns banging. Three hundred yards sepa-
rated them now as Crow and his men rode up to the
narrow gap in the adobe wall.

Johnson flew from his saddle before his roan bounded
to a halt. Running, half stumbling, he reached the latch
and swung the gate open. A bullet struck the dried mud
just as Crow was hurrying his horse through, kicking up
a spit of dust and sand. Flinching over the closeness of the
shot, Crow ducked down inside his shirt collar and rode
through the opening with Middleton close on his heels.
Seconds later Johnson appeared, clinging to the back of
his horse with his rifle clutched in one hand.

"This way!" Crow shouted, sending the gray eastward in an all out run, leaning low in the saddle when another burst of steady gunfire came from the village. Flying lead sizzled over the top of the wall as they rode hard to make a circle around Hidalgo.

Middleton aimed an angry look over his shoulder. "The sorry sons of bitches shot my pardner," he growled, hard to hear above the thunder of galloping hooves. "I'm gonna make the bastards pay if they get close enough . . ."

Beyond the walled village they could see the broad valley running north and the road that would take them back to Texas. Gritting his teeth, Crow clamped his legs to the gray's sides and prepared himself to make the ride of his life.

Chapter 19

Their horses were laboring by the time they reached the far side of the valley. Lather clung to the geldings' coats. Behind them, trailing along in a boiling cloud of caliche, almost a dozen men charged after them, but there was no shooting now, for the range was too great for any accuracy. Along the rim of the valley they could see cavalrymen in blue tunics exhanging gunfire with scattered remnants of Cortez's army. Some of the *federale* soldiers had broken off to ride to the valley floor on a line that would put them across the path of Zambrano's *pistoleros*.

Crow's gray was first to climb the steep grade out of the valley. Nostrils flared, their horses struggled for wind while their strides shortened. At the top of the trail, Crow chanced a look backward when a sudden staccato of gunshots erupted down below. Zambrano's men were firing at the *federales*, and the shots were being returned. The skirmish would buy Crow and his men precious time. He slowed the exhausted gray to a trot when Johnson and Middleton came alongside him.

"Let 'em blow a minute or two," he said, booting his rifle below a stirrup leather, still watching the fight in the

valley until they rode out of sight where the trail made a
bend. He gave the others a weak grin. "We got the
money, boys. Damn near got killed, but we got the loot."
He looked to Middleton. "Sorry about Roy," he added
quietly. "You'll get his share of the reward I'm paying,
just in case he's got any next of kin."

Middleton glanced back; then he shook his head.
"Never did hear Roy mention no family. Besides that, we
ain't out of this fix just yet. It's still a hell of a long way to
the Rio Grande, an' you know it well as me."

"We've got ourselves a good lead right now," Crow
offered, watching the trail in front of them. "It's up to us
to see that it stays that way. We're mounted on the best
horses if I'm any judge of horseflesh. All we've gotta do is
make sure they don't make a move when we ain't ready."

Johnson was staring thoughtfully down their backtrail.
"I figure that for a spell, they'll have their hands full with
them *federales*. But if'n the truth got told, we've got just as
much to fear from those Mexican soldiers as we do Zambrano. If either one of them bunches come after us, we're
in for a runnin' fight plumb to the border."

Middleton frowned. "Maybe they'll both be too busy
fightin' each other to chase us down."

"That's a notion I wouldn't put much stock in," Crow
said, eyeing the four bags of money hanging from Johnson's saddle horn, remembering the warning given by
Clint Sikes that none of the men he hired could be trusted.
If Johnson made up his mind to do a double cross somewhere farther along the trail, he could simply ride off with
more than half of the bank loot. Four sacks filled with
currency would be enough to tempt a man on the run
from the law such as Lee Johnson.

Starting down a gentle grade, Crow reined his horse

over to Johnson's roan without slowing from a ground-eating trot. "I'll hang those bags from my saddle now," he said.

Johnson grunted and handed first one pair, then the other two bags over to Crow without uttering a word. Crow tied two sacks behind the cantle, securing them with his saddle strings until he noticed Middleton was watching him closely.

"You don't trust either one of us," he said coldly.

"Never said that," Crow replied. "I'm the one responsible for this here money. It stays with me until we get to Laredo. You'll get what's coming to you, but nothing more."

Middleton's expression hardened. "We done risked our necks for that money. Cost Roy his life, too. Don't forget what you said about handin' me my pardner's share . . ."

They rode across a dry ravine in silence. Off in the distance they could hear the pop of guns. For now, Crow began to relax a little after the close brushes with death back at the village. His heartbeat slowed, although in the back of his brain something assured him that their troubles were far from over.

Climbing out of the ravine, Crow looked south and found no sign of pursuit on the horizon. "We're gaining more time," he said under his breath, holding his horse in a steady trot. "If we've got any luck at all, those *federales* will keep Zambrano occupied."

"Unless," Johnson said, sounding tired, "them soldiers decide to come after us themselves. Could be we'll have both bunches doggin' our trail pretty soon, if we ain't all that lucky to start with. Never was all that lucky myself, most times. I make it a habit not to count on Lady Luck.

Seems like she's made a practice of makin' life miserable for Lee Johnson. Damned if she ain't tested me whenever she could."

To the south, the gunfire died down to an occasional shot. To the west, the sun lowered near the horizon. North, purple shadows deepened where the road passed close to the mountains. Facing a long night in the saddle, Crow steeled himself for the hours ahead.

Once, he reminded himself that he was flanked by two men who would kill him for the money he carried, should he grow careless. In the dark, one or the other could easily find the opportunity to gun him down from the rear.

The night was as black as pitch. Pale stars shed little light into the dark passes, and the moon had not yet risen. The clatter of hooves broke the eerie silence around them as they pushed their horses northward at a trot. Now and then, Crow signaled a halt to study their backtrail and listen for the sounds of pursuit. Hardly a word had been said since they left the valley. The silence suited Crow's mood right then. With the coming of full dark his nerves had grown raw-edged. Whenever he could he kept both Johnson and Middleton where he could see them, being careful to avoid giving them a shot at his backside. His suspicions had grown since nightfall that one or the other would make a play for the fortune he carried on the gray, wondering which man would betray him. All along he had known that a time might come when men of their breed would be tempted by so much money. That time had arrived. Worn down by their ordeal in Hidalgo, he fought off sleep and did his best to stay alert, ready for the first sign of treachery. And always there was the knowledge that behind them Luis Zambrano and some of his best *pistoleros* might be closing the gap between them. Or what could be worse, a squad of mounted *federales* could be on their trail riding better horses.

On a ridge where the road ended a climb, Crow halted his horse and turned back in the saddle. All three winded geldings gasped for air during the pause.

"Don't see a thing," he said softly, scanning the dark slopes and ravines behind them. He gathered his reins and prepared to ride off, when from the corner of his eye, he saw a slight movement that made his blood run cold. Middleton had drawn his pistol, aiming for Crow's chest, starlight gleaming from the barrel of his Colt. In a flash Crow knew he was much too late to draw his own weapon, caught off guard when he paid close attention to the road south. He dove for the ground just as the quiet ended with a mighty roar. The clap of exploding gunpowder sent the horses into motion at once, lunging away from the sudden noise.

He fell on his chest with a grunt, clawing for his revolver, wondering how the bounty hunter could have missed at point-blank range. Then another body tumbled to the ground as horses scrambled for footing on the rocks. There was a groan and the acrid smell of gunsmoke before the echo of the gunshot faded away. He swung his pistol up, dumbfounded by the turn of events. How could Middleton have missed? Who had fallen from the horse?

Blinking from the shock of his fall, Crow's vision slowly cleared. He saw Lee Johnson aboard his horse attempting to calm the roan in the aftermath of the explosion. Middleton lay a few yards away, sprawled on his back, groaning, his legs working back and forth as though he were trying to run. Light from the stars glinted off the gun in

Johnson's fist, and then Crow understood. His fingers relaxed around the Colt. He took a deep breath as Johnson rode over to Crow's gray gelding to pick up the reins, holstering his pistol before he leaned out of the saddle.

Johnson rode up with the gray in tow. "He was aimin' to shoot you whilst your back was turned, lawman. Wasn't time to yell a warnin'. Had to kill him afore he killed you. I been thinkin' all along he wanted that money for hisself."

Crow got to his feet slowly, still shaken by the gunshot and the fall. He dropped his gun back in its holster while looking down at Middleton briefly. "I owe you my life, Lee," he said in a hoarse, faraway voice. "I guessed something like this could happen. I tried to be ready for it . . . kept my eyes on the two of you best I could."

The wounded man emitted a louder moan, though now his feet were stilled as he clutched a dark stain spreading over the front of his shirt.

"Can't say as I blame you for havin' me figured the same as him," Johnson said, resting an elbow on his saddle horn, thumbing back the brim of his hat. "I ain't no backshooter. I reckon you'll have to take my word for it."

Crow let out a whispering sigh. "You could have killed me just now and ridden off with all the money. You had the opportunity and you didn't take it, so I reckon that's good enough for me." He walked over to Middleton and stared down into his pain-ridden eyes. "He ain't dead yet. Fetch his horse for me. I can't stomach just leaving him here to die. We'll try to get him to a doctor in Laredo if he can make it that far."

"He ain't gonna live that long," Johnson replied, wagging his head. "Don't make any sense to have him slow us down. He jus' tried to kill you, if you'll recall."

"Just the same, I can't leave him here. Fetch me that horse. I'll do what I can for him."

"You're too damn softhearted, lawman. I say you oughta let the bastard die right where he is."

Crow shook his head. "Some men ain't made that way, Lee. I saw plenty of suffering in the war. Maybe the bounty hunter deserves to die for what he tried to do, but my conscience won't allow me to ride off and leave him like this. I'd be obliged if you'd bring me his horse."

"Suit yourself," Johnson said, almost a whisper, lifting his reins. "I'll lay odds he won't go a mile afore he draws his last breath. Won't sorrow me none. Never did have no use for a damn bounty hunter in the first place. You won't catch me grievin' over him passin' on."

Crow bent down to take Middleton's pistol from the ground beside the dying man. He stuck it in the waistband of his pants, thinking how close he'd come to feeling the sting of one of the bullets. Lee Johnson's deadly fast draw and sure aim had spared him.

The bounty hunter's eyes followed Crow as he leaned over to take the gun. His breathing was ragged, irregular now.

"That damn nigra's . . . gonna do . . . the same to you," Middleton gasped, snarling when he said it, then wincing when the effort to speak pained him more.

Johnson rode back with the bounty hunter's horse before Crow answered. "I'll bet against it," he said, examining the bloody hole in Middleton's chest as more blood poured from the dying man's fingers. "Some men have a little dash of honor in them, Bill, something you'd know nothing about. Lee could have killed me just now, but he didn't. I'll sleep a little better after tonight, if we get any sleep at all, knowing Lee is watching my backside. Can't say I ever felt the same way when my back was turned on you."

A wet, gurgling sound came from Middleton's throat, and his eyes turned glassy.

"Don't trouble yourself liftin' him to the saddle," Johnson said quietly. "He'll be passin' on in a moment or two. I seen that look on men's faces afore. He ain't long fer this place."

"You're probably right," Crow said, taking another deep breath, glancing to the south. "We'll wait here a spell . . ."

Middleton coughed suddenly. His limbs stiffened; then there was silence when his chest no longer moved. Somewhere in the night, an owl hooted. One of the horses snorted softly and swished its tail, somehow sensing the arrival of death.

Johnson swung down from the saddle and reached into each of the dead man's pockets, puzzling Crow briefly until he explained. "No sense leavin' any money on him. Where he's headed now, he damn sure can't spend any of it."

Dawn brightened the eastern sky as they neared the pass where Captain Cortez had tried to ambush them. Early buzzards floated above the cliff where bodies lay among the rocks, following the airborne scent of decomposing flesh to the victims of Johnson's Remington. There had been no sign of pursuit along their backtrail during the night. When they stopped on high ground to listen for hoofbeats, there was only silence. Johnson led Middleton's gelding as they rode into the mouth of the pass. Keeping the horse as a spare helped Crow worry less about one of the other animals coming up lame.

As they rounded a bend that would take them down a gradual slope into a narrow ravine, Crow halted his horse and stood in the stirrups for a look behind them. His eyes narrowed suddenly when he saw a tiny movement on the horizon. "There they are," he said, his voice trailing off.

Johnson frowned, watching the same spot. "Can't tell who it is. Or how many."

"Time we pushed these horses, Lee. It's still a hell of a long ride across these mountains. Then there's that desert before we get to the river. We can't afford to miss that waterhole at the foot of the trail where it starts up from the flats. Let's ride."

Chapter 20

Galloping, then resting their mounts at a walk, they rode until noon under a blistering sun that drained reserves from the horses much too quickly. Crow's gray fared better than the roan, while Middleton's horse traveled more easily without the weight of a rider. On a ridge with a view to the south, Johnson changed horses during a brief rest. Continually looking backward, both men held an uneasy silence for a time until Johnson pointed to a speck in the distance moving along the rutted trail.

"They're still comin'. We ain't gained no ground on 'em, but it don't appear we lost any. Wish we knowed which bunch it is back there."

"It's Zambrano," Crow said, sounding as tired as he felt after a night without sleep. "He's the only one who knows about the money. I'm guessing he fought his way around those *federales* to come after the bank bags. Could be the *federales* are behind him . . ."

Johnson took off his hat to sleeve sweat from his face. He nodded. "This heat'll be hell on the hosses this afternoon if we keep ridin' this hard. Don't suppose we got much choice. By now, whoever's back there knows it's just the two of us, after they found the bounty hunter's body. I figure it'll make 'em come harder, make 'em reckless, knowin' there ain't but two men to handle in a fight. We got ourselves in a hoss race now. It ain't gonna be over 'til we reach that river."

Crow patted Dixie's neck affectionately. It pained him to use his favorite horse the way he was. "This ol' gray always had plenty of stamina. But like me, he's getting a bit long in the tooth to be put to the test. Hate like hell to do it to him."

The horses' flanks were still heaving when they rode off the ridge at a trot. Just once more, Crow glanced backward, hooding his eyes to keep out the sun. The men following them had begun a snakelike descent down the side of a mountain, and now, they seemed closer than before.

Side by side, they kicked their horses to a lope. Crow settled against the cantle, ignoring sore muscles, fighting his growing fatigue. Their lives would depend on the animals they rode and keen senses over the last part of a long trail back to Texas. Yet try as he might to stay alert, his mind grew numb. He looked over at Johnson. "My head's getting fuzzy. Maybe it's the heat."

Johnson gave him a one-sided grin. "You'll wake up in one hell of a hurry if they catch up to us. Nothin' like duckin' hot lead to wake a feller up. This wouldn't be the right time to doze off in the saddle. Might cost you another hole in your hat, lawman."

"The name's Jim Ed. Down here, I don't work for the law."

Something Crow said made Johnson's face turn hard. He sent a steely look in Crow's direction. "If you're aimin' to try to arrest me when we get close to the border, put the notion out of your head. I'm faster with a gun. I'd hate to have to kill you, but I damn sure will if you try to take me back."

Despite his weariness, Crow cleared his thoughts to explain his intentions. "It never crossed my mind and that's the honest truth," he said, raising his voice to be heard above the galloping hooves. "What you did before we met is your affair. But there's something stronger than that. You saved my life when the bounty hunter drew on me, and that's a debt I can never repay. I owe you. Will for the rest of my days. Rest easy. I'd never try to take you back to stand trial. It ain't in me to do that to a friend, no matter what you done to break the law."

Johnson seemed satisfied. He shook his head and then looked over his shoulder, squinting in the sun's fierce glare. "I can see their dust. Better make some time whilst we can still see 'em, if we don't kill these hosses doin' it."

They urged their horses to a faster run when they struck a stretch of level ground. Crow watched Dixie's ears, feeling the rhythm of the big gelding's run beneath him. He had always despised men who used horses cruelly, and now he was guilty of it himself. Thus he tried to close his mind to what he was doing to a good animal, considering the consequences if he allowed the gray to rest.

They made the spring just before nightfall. Their horses stumbled down the last half mile of the slope where the trail dropped to the vast, dry prairie. When they reached the tiny pool both men dropped to the ground and loosened their cinches. The gray buried its muzzle below the surface to drink, and only then did Crow kneel down to cup water in his hands. His head was reeling from lack of sleep. His limbs trembled with weakness as he held the water to his lips. Johnson squatted down across the pool to drink and splash water on his face and chest. Between gulps of water, the horses gasped for air, flanks heaving.

"We'll kill our mounts if we keep this up," Crow said between mouthfuls. "Zambrano's horses won't fare any better. I say we take it slower tonight, so we'll have something left in our animals when the sun comes up."

"Takin' it slow could get us killed," Johnson replied, looking up the mountain, following the road with his eyes.

"We'll be just as dead if we're afoot in this desert. I can't stomach punishing the horses like this."

"You've got a soft spot for hosses, ain't you?"

"Always did favor an honest horse. Most of my life I've been depending on a horse, so it's natural to develop a liking for the good ones."

"They's jus' animals," Johnson said matter-of-factly, with a shrug of his powerful shoulders.

Crow let it drop. Nothing short of imminent death would make him use Dixie any harder than he had today. "I've got some jerky in my saddlebags. Maybe we'd both feel better with something in our belly."

"This water feels mighty nice," the gunman replied, grinning. "But I reckon some of that dried meat will do tolerable well. Too bad we ain't got some of that whiskey. It was on the mule . . ."

"Not all of it," Crow said, remembering the pint he put with his spare shirt. "Wish I'd remembered it sooner." He stood up on stiffened legs and walked to his saddlebags with a pronounced limp to retrieve the bottle. When he pulled the cork, sweet barley vapors from the neck of the bottle made him smile with anticipation. The whiskey burned down his throat in a single gulp that brought tears to his eyes.

He passed the pint to Johnson and cast a lingering look across the purple prairie they must cross to reach Texas. Even in the cool of late evening, the dry land looked unforgiving. "By my rough guesswork, we've got seventy or eighty hard miles in front of us. There's a whole townful of people back in Carrizo Springs who're hoping we can make it across that stretch with their money."

"You know, lawman, you gotta be half-crazy," Johnson said after he took a bubbling swallow from the bottle. "Most county sheriffs don't make more'n twenty a month. For a twenty-dollar-a-month job, you risked gettin' killed, makin' a fool's play by goin' to Mexico to get stolen money back. Some would say you been out in the sun too long, to try a stunt like this all by your lonesome. You talk like a man who's got good sense, but you damn sure don't act like one."

"The people of Carrizo Springs are my friends. They looked to me to protect the money they saved. When the bank got robbed, they lost everything . . . a life's work for some. I couldn't just sit there and do nothing about it. I had to try something. Besides, I didn't do it by myself. You were there to help me, and so was Roy Hyde, and Bill Middleton."

Johnson appeared to be examining the contents of the bottle for a time. "I figure they planned all along to gun you down if you got the money back."

"Maybe. I don't suppose I'll ever know . . ."

The gunman stood up abruptly, looking south, scowling at the darkening road. "Got this feelin' they're gettin' close to us. If we intend to keep them bags of money, we'd better hit our saddles an' ride hard as we can. I know you got feelin's for that dappled gray hoss, but you'd better forget 'em for a spell an' make him cover some ground in a hurry."

"Let's fill our canteens and give the horses another five minutes or they'll drop dead right underneath us."

Johnson took another mouthful of whiskey and corked the bottle, handing it back to Crow. "If somethin' has to drop dead, I'd sure as hell rather it was a hoss. But we'll do like you say an' wait a spell longer. Tonight, I'm gonna ride the roan. He's rested some."

Crow took down the canteens and filled each to the top, thinking how precious the water would seem tomorrow in the middle of the desert. Dusk darkened the prairie, deepening shadows below the mesquites and brush. Gazing across the land, he knew how difficult the crossing would be on trail-weary, thirsty horses. Both he and Johnson had been without sleep too long, facing another night and day of sleeplessness. Hanging the canteens from their saddle horns, his arms and legs felt like lead weights. When the task was finished he took another drink of whiskey and felt somewhat better before mounting the gray.

Reining away from the spring, he scanned the road behind them. "Maybe their horses played out," he said wishfully as they trotted away from the pool.

Johnson merely grunted. By the expression on his face, he was doubtful about it.

In the cooler air of night the horses traveled easily over the first few miles of level ground. Here and there, feeding rattlesnakes crawled across the wagon ruts, forcing the men wide of the trail. Full dark came, and it was impossible to see what lay behind them for any distance. The road lay empty as far as they could see in both directions, walled on either side by thick stands of cholla, Spanish dagger, yucca and cactus, and the ever-present mesquite trees no taller than a man. Night birds whistled alarm when the riders approached. Now and then an owl hooted from a distant mesquite limb. At night the prairie looked deceptively peaceful, serene, causing Crow's eyelids to grow heavy. Time and again he caught himself dozing off in the saddle no matter how hard he tried to stay awake.

"I can't keep my eyes open," he told Johnson as they crossed a gentle swell in the brushland at a trot.

Johnson looked over his shoulder. He seemed unusually edgy now. "This ain't the time to fall off that hoss. Can't see nothin' back there, but I can feel 'em comin'. I get this feelin' down the back of my neck when there's trouble headed my way."

Crow shook his head to clear it. "I sure hope your neck is wrong this time. I can't see to shoot with my eyes stuck shut."

Johnson chuckled dryly. "They'll pop open soon as the shootin' starts. I'd be grateful for some more of that whiskey right about now."

Crow removed the pint from his back pocket and handed it across. "I'd be just as grateful if you didn't get drunk on me tonight. One of us has to keep a clear head, and it sure as hell won't be me, tired as I am."

"Ain't much danger of me gettin' drunk, Jim Ed, not with a gang of Mexican gunmen on the loose somewheres behind us. There ain't enough whiskey in Texas to get me loop-legged drunk out here."

* * *

Near midnight, with a piece of moon lighting the brush, they stopped on a tiny knoll to study their backtrail. Suddenly, as Crow was straining to see in the distance, Johnson stood in his stirrups and pointed south.

"Yonder they are!" he said coldly, his voice like dry sand. "We been travelin' too slow. They've gained considerable on us."

"Damn," Crow growled when he saw dark shapes moving along the ruts. "Don't see how they could have done it. We're riding better horses . . . I just know it."

Johnson said nothing for half a minute more, intent upon the riders. "If my eyes ain't playin' tricks on me, I see how they caught up so quick. Half them hosses back there have got empty saddles. They brought along spares, knowin' they could ride us down when ours played out by makin' a change. They been savin' their hosses, changin' every hour or two. Got to hand it to Zambrano. He's plenty smart when it comes to this dry country."

A sinking feeling awakened in the pit of Crow's stomach. Zambrano's tactics made perfect sense. "They'll be in shooting distance by morning if they keep this up. A good marksman can pick us off one at a time. Our horses will be too far gone to outrun them. And there damn sure ain't anyplace for us to take cover out here."

"Maybe," Johnson said, a different tone in his voice now. "If that's what they aim to do, maybe I got the cure for it hangin' from my saddle . . ."

"Your Remington!" Crow exclaimed, remembering the long-range shots fired at the pass. "With that cannon of yours, you can drop them before they get in range with their rifles."

"Might work," he said. "Trouble is, I ain't got many shells left. Most of the ammunition was aboard our mule.

Looked in my saddlebags a while back, jus' passin' time.
Counted hardly ten cartridges . . . maybe it was nine."

Crow's brief exhilaration passed quickly. "Nine won't
be enough, will it? Not unless you can make every shot
count, and then we'll have to get lucky if there are any of
them left."

"We're wastin' time," Johnson said, wheeling his horse
off the knoll with Middleton's gelding in tow.

They struck a lope down moonlit ruts, turning around
often to watch the riders behind them.

Chapter 21

Dixie's strides had begun to falter. Crow knew the big dappled gelding couldn't hold a lope any longer without rest. In the hours before daylight he'd closed his mind to what he was doing to a trusted animal. It was a case of terrible choices, to save his own life and the money belonging to the citizens of Carrizo Springs, or spare his horse. Listening to Dixie gasp for wind under the punishment of a rider's heels was pure agony for Crow, yet the alternative was to stand and fight a band of hard *pistoleros* bent on killing him for the money he carried. There was really no choice to be made; he had to keep pushing the horse as hard as he could.

False dawn paled the eastern sky, illuminating the brushland. Now they could see clearly the men following them. A count revealed there were eight riders, each leading a spare mount. Zambrano had known what it would take to ride down the men from Texas before he left Hidalgo. He came prepared for a long, hard chase to the border, for he knew the land they must cross, its harsh secrets. Once, as the sun came above the horizon, Crow watched them change horses in the middle of the road.

Men in dusty sombreros jumped from one saddle to another in less time than it took to tell about it.

The distance between them was now down to less than a mile, a mile of thorny wasteland as flat as a frying pan, sliced by an arrow-straight road heading due north. Off to the south, the dim outline of the mountains loomed above the desert. Caliche dust curled away from the flying heels of the horses, those belonging to Zambrano and his men, and the three weary geldings bearing Crow, Johnson, and an empty saddle toward safety in Texas. The spare horse could mean the difference between life and death, should Dixie or the roan pull up lame.

The desert locusts had begun their piercing cries at dawn, and the sound was a constant drone in the riders' ears, a reminder that the land they were in was unfit for all but the most hardy creatures who could survive without water. Surrounded by the shrill screams of the *chichadas,* Crow and the black gunman who had saved his life raced for the Rio Grande aboard laboring, gaunt-flanked horses.

"Got to stop for a minute!" Crow shouted, slowing the gray after two brutal hours of galloping, then trotting their horses in the morning heat.

Johnson turned back in the saddle. "They're too close," he cried above the din of locusts and drumming hooves. "If we stop, they'll be in shootin' range afore we know it. Damn it, Jim Ed! Stop feelin' sorry for that hoss!"

"He'll go down," Crow argued, hearing a change in Dixie's hoofbeats. "We've got to fight them sometime— get them off our backs for a spell. Now's as good a time as any. Load that rifle and let's pick a spot where we'll have a little cover."

Johnson drew the Remington from his saddle boot. He

took a handful of cartridges from a saddlebag and put them in his shirt pocket. His roan gelding had begun to wheeze, sucking badly needed air through its flared nostrils. Coated with lather, the horse had fared no better than Dixie during the night. Now, both animals were near complete exhaustion, moving in shortened strides that warned of a fall should anything unfamiliar appear suddenly in the trail, a stretch of uneven ground or a rock.

Ahead, Crow sighted a thin stand of larger mesquites to one side of the road. "There!" he yelled, pointing to the trees.

They rode up to the mesquites and pulled rein. Dixie's sides were heaving . . . wind whistled through his muzzle in short, steady bursts. Johnson's roan lowered its head, gasping, sweat dripping from its neck and shoulders to form little damp circles in the caliche ruts. Both men dropped to the ground, Crow with his Winchester, Johnson with the big bore Remington held loosely to his shoulder as he flipped up the swing sight and then sent a shell into the firing chamber.

"Wait 'til you're sure of a target," Crow said, squinting into heat waves dancing above the road where the shapes of men and galloping horses moved below a swirl of yellow-white dust.

"I don't need no shootin' lessons, Jim Ed. I'll allow for the drop when they get close enough. Meantime, you busy yourself givin' them hosses some of that water in the crown of your hat. I reckon you'll have to put a finger in them bullet holes to keep it from runnin' out afore it gets drunk."

"Hand me yours," Crow said, wiping sweat from his face with a forearm.

Johnson gave Crow the hat; then he sighted along the

rifle barrel, closing one eye. He spread his legs slightly to allow for the kick and waited, holding his breath.

Crow took a canteen and poured water into the hat. Dixie smelled water and immediately drank all of it, only a few swallows. As he watered the roan Crow glanced to the approaching riders and felt his heartbeat quicken. They made a fearsome sight, eight men in dusty sombreros with cartridge belts across their chests, galloping toward them relentlessly along a two-rut road. He had survived an all-out battle in Hidalgo with these men, only to face them again in the middle of an arid wasteland where there was no cover, no protection of any kind. During the bank robbery, he'd had places to hide from which he could shoot. His first encounter with them had only cost him a nick in the leg; the second fight he'd gotten away without a scratch. This time, he couldn't count on being so lucky. Eight guns would be blazing away at him, and he would be out in the open, a sitting duck. It seemed he had been fighting Zambrano and his *pistoleros* forever, a war that would not end until one side or the other had been annihilated.

The Mexicans rode harder now, bunched together, leaning over their horses' necks. Rifle barrels glistened with sunlight. The distance was down to half a mile— closing quickly. He could hear the faint drum of the horses' hooves, sounding like the first rumble of an approaching rainstorm. He tossed the empty canteen aside and picked up his Winchester, knowing the range was much too great but feeling better with his hands wrapped around the stock of a gun. He slowly levered a shell into the firing chamber and passed his tongue over dry, suncracked lips without taking his eyes from the horsemen. Leaving the horses ground-hitched, he walked up beside

Johnson in the scant shade of a mesquite tree and spoke
in a gravelly voice.

"Don't wait too damn long, Lee. I'm getting a case of
the shakes already. Hell of a sight, eight gunmen headed
our way bent on killing us. A man don't ever forget
something like this if he lives to be a hundred . . ."

"If I had a few more shells, I could slow 'em down a bit
by killin' three or four of their hosses."

"I'd just as soon you didn't do it like that."

Steadying the rifle against his shoulder, Johnson made
a sound that was something like a laugh. "You got a
tender heart for a lawman, Jim Ed. Don't fret over it
none. I ain't hardly got enough bullets in the first place.
It was jus' an idea."

Now the riders were very close, a quarter mile and
narrowing the gap quickly.

"Hang on to them hosses," Johnson said quietly.
"When this thing goes off it makes one hell of a racket."

Crow hurried to the horses and gathered the reins,
glancing over his shoulder, wondering when Johnson
would take his first shot, for it appeared the riders were in
range now.

"Wonder what he's waiting for," Crow whispered to
himself.

An answer came suddenly, the clap of igniting gunpowder, an ear-splitting roar that made Johnson take a half
step back when he felt the recoil against his shoulder. The
whine of speeding lead accompanied the gunshot. Johnson quickly adjusted the Vernier swing sight and chambered another round. All eight riders continued their
charge—the shot was a miss.

"Goddamn Creedmore," Johnson muttered, sighting

down the barrel again. "Makes me wonder if the barrel ain't crooked."

A second shot bellowed from the mouth of the gun. Middleton's horse snorted and pulled back on the reins. At the front of the pack of horsemen, a *pistolero* flipped off the rump of his mount, tumbling into a ball before he fell out of sight beneath the horses' hooves.

"Got him," Johnson said, working the mechanism to eject the spent cartridge. The brass casing dropped between Johnson's boots, still smoldering.

The riders continued at a full gallop. An answering shot popped in the distance; Crow could see the muzzle flash and a wisp of smoke coming from the barrel of a rifle.

A third shot roared from Johnson's gun. A huge .50–.70 slug whispered through the air. Then a running horse collapsed as though it struck a gopher hole, pitching its rider forward with arms windmilling until the man dropped out of sight in the dust.

"Too low. Didn't mean to hit the hoss. Don't leave but six," Johnson said needlessly. Crow was keeping his own careful tally.

The charge was broken. Sombrero-clad riders drew back on their horses' reins. Two gunshots cracked from the group of men gathered in the middle of the road. Somewhere high above Crow's head, a bullet sped harmlessly off into the brush.

"That'll hold 'em for a spell," Johnson said, wheeling around to trot over to his horse.

"Not for long," Crow predicted, watching the man who had fallen from his horse scramble to his feet. He got up and ran toward the group of riders to mount a spare horse as Crow swung over his saddle. "The one who lost his horse is back in the chase, so the count is seven now."

Johnson took his hat off the saddle horn and placed it on his head before swinging aboard the roan. "Ain't got but six bullets left for this here rifle," he muttered, watching the Mexicans mill about in the road, uncertain what to do about Johnson's long-range gun. "Looks like we bought ourselves a little more time."

Heeling their horses to a trot, they left the tiny mesquite thicket and continued north. At the same time, Zambrano and his men moved forward again.

"They're gonna stalk us," Crow said, looking back. "Wait for the right place, the right time to close in."

"Let 'em come," Johnson said savagely, his expression changed, his eyes becoming mere slits when he looked at the men behind them. "They're liable to find out ol' Lee Johnson ain't all that easy to kill. Plenty of folks tried it, includin' that pair of bushwhackin' bounty hunters, an' I still ain't got any holes in this black hide of mine. I'm gettin' real tired of havin' this bunch of Mexicans on my tail."

Crow heard the change in his voice and noted the difference in his countenance. Not even when he'd warned Crow about attempting to take him back to Texas had there been such a look of hatred on his face. Crow had almost forgotten that Lee Johnson was a wanted killer, a paid gun.

The Mexicans charged again when a gentle rise in the brushland came between them. Dust boiled higher into the sky as they sent their horses into a full gallop.

"Here the bastards come," Johnson said, wheeling his roan around to face the charge. He dropped to the ground with his rifle and handed his reins to Crow. Raising the Vernier, he squinted down the sights and grew still.

To make less of a target, Crow jumped down and drew the Winchester, wondering why the Mexicans had chosen this place to fight. Steadying the rifle on the seat of his saddle, he stood behind Dixie and waited with his teeth clenched. Sweat fell from his hatband, and he ignored it, intent upon the coming riders. In the distance, men and horses grew larger. Again, he listened to the rumble of flying hooves.

The Remington exploded, spooking the horses. A *pistolero* at the front of the charge left his saddle, gripping his chest as he let his rifle fall to the ground. It was a near-perfect shot at an almost impossible range. Crow shook his head in admiration. Not even during four bloody years of war had he seen such marksmanship.

The loss of another man at such tremendous distance brought the Mexicans' charge to an abrupt halt. They sat their horses, talking among themselves. When Johnson saw this, he turned around and smiled. "This Creedmore is makin' 'em think again afore they ride straight at us. Don't reckon they know I'm damn near out of ammunition." He hurried to his horse and swung up, wearing a look of satisfaction. "We're gonna make it to that big river, Jim Ed, if they don't figure out I'm runnin' out of shells for this here gun."

Crow looked north, guessing the distance to the border. With no more delays they might make it by nightfall. "Let's make some tracks, Lee. I'm hoping Zambrano hasn't got any tricks up his sleeve. As long as we can see them, I figure we'll be okay. But the land changes a little up yonder . . . a few hills, more trees and gullies. Maybe that's what they aim to do—keep pushing us 'til we get to

a spot where they can ride a circle around us without
being seen."

They were off again at a lope, forcing weary horses to
travel faster through the worst heat of the day. Now the
desert would become a more dangerous adversary, waiting to claim the footsore, exhausted geldings they rode.

Chapter 22

As Crow knew it would, the land had begun a subtle change. To the north, low hills and winding ravines offered too many hiding places for men bent on an ambush. Zambrano and his men, riding fresher horses, stood a chance of being able to flank them and cut them off. The odds were now six against two. The sun hung like a fiery orange ball above the western hills, baking the land, sapping the horses' strength. Zambrano was showing more caution now, after losing two men to Johnson's Remington. He was hanging back, safely out of range, waiting for the right opportunity.

Glancing to the sky, Crow figured there were still four or five hours of daylight left, hours of merciless heat, the river nowhere in sight on the distant horizon. The two horses could barely manage to hold a trot now, traveling with heads lowered, muzzles almost touching the ground, each stride seemingly a little shorter. Zambrano's advantage was building. His men had rested horses when the time came for them to close in for the kill. And the land offered protection if they spread out to ride a circle around their quarry.

Despite numbing fatigue after so many sleepless hours in a saddle, Crow grew suddenly angry as he saw their chances of escape slipping away. "I'll be goddamn if I'll let 'em have this money back!" he cried, turning around in the saddle to watch the Mexicans, balling his hands into fists. "Let the sons of bitches come! Some of them are damn sure gonna die when they try it, and by God, I swear I'm gonna kill Luis Zambrano this time if I get the chance! He's making this personal, and he's gonna goddamn sure be sorry he ever tangled with Jim Ed Crow!"

"Take it easy, Jim Ed," Johnson said quietly. "No call to get yourself all riled up jus' yet. Drink the last of that whiskey an' calm yourself 'til the shootin' starts."

Crow bit down hard and closed his eyes for a moment, battling the swell of rage inside him. He took out the pint and eyed its shallow contents; then he pulled the cork with his teeth and spit it away. "Take a swig," he said, handing the bottle to Johnson, speaking softer now.

Johnson took a mouthful and gave the pint back. Crow emptied it with a single swallow and tossed the bottle into the brush. A stretch of hills lay before them where the yucca and cactus were more widely scattered, where the mesquites were farther apart.

"This could be where they try to ride around us," he said, glancing back, his anger gone, replaced by the beginnings of fear. "If I was Zambrano, this is where I'd spread my men out on either flank. With our horses plumb spent, there ain't a damn thing we can do about it if that's what they do."

"You could be right," Johnson agreed, scanning the hills and ravines ahead. "One thing's for sure, they ain't gonna follow us all the way to the river."

Johnson's roan started to cough, traveling with its muzzle lowered."

"Time you changed horses," Crow said. "That strawberry roan won't go much farther." He looked down at Dixie's ears. Although the gray fared somewhat better, he knew the horse was all but finished. Again, he closed his mind to the cruelty of it and thought about the forthcoming battle with the *pistoleros*. He could see it in his mind's eye, the Mexicans circling them, lying in wait for their adversaries behind a hill, perhaps hidden in a dry wash. Zambrano had outsmarted him, employing better tactics at just the right time. Replacing the anger of moments before, Crow felt overwhelmed by a sense of despair. The Mexicans would surely kill him and Johnson to get the money back. The citizens of Carrizo Springs would never know just how close he had come to returning their money to them.

The road crossed a hilltop. To the east and west, the trail was surrounded by rolling hills and shallow gullies, perfect places to hide for a bushwhacking. Crow had failed to consider what the final miles of land would be like when he'd formed his plan to rob Zambrano back at Hidlago. Worse, he hadn't figured on bringing along spare horses, and now his shortsightedness was about to be their undoing.

"They're movin'," Johnson warned, "jus' like you figured they would."

Crow whirled around in the saddle. Four of Zambrano's *pistoleros* were leaving the road, two to the east, another pair to the west. They galloped off into sparse brush to begin a deadly circle around him and Johnson. Zambrano, aboard his big black horse, remained in the road with a lone *pistolero*. The game of cat and mouse was over. The killing would begin very soon.

"Damn," Crow whispered, pulling his rifle to check the loading tube. His pistol held six cartridges; thus he was as prepared as he ever would be for the coming fight. He shook his head angrily. "Looks like they got us, Lee. These horses ain't got a drop of stamina left."

Johnson had changed to the spare gelding. His fresh mount stood a chance of outrunning the Mexicans' horses, but Dixie was finished, having nothing left.

"You can try to save your own skin," Crow said when Johnson had nothing to say. "I'll pay you the rest of what I owe you, and you can make a run for the river . . . couldn't say as I'd blame you."

It seemed an odd time for the black gunman to smile. "I ain't goin' no place," he said after showing off his teeth. "I come this far, so I believe I'll stay to see the end of it. I know you've got me figured for a man without no principles, on account of me bein' wanted by the law. But the truth is, we ain't all that different, you an' me. I took the wrong fork in the trail some years back, an' I 'spect I'll pay for it the rest of my days. Always tried to keep my word the way my pappy done, an' I gave you my word that I'd see this through. So I'm stayin' 'til we reach the river—if we get that far."

"I'm surprised," Crow replied. "I reckon there's a lesson in this . . . that there are good men on both sides of the law these days. Hard times can force good men make bad choices, I suppose."

The four *pistoleros* galloped wide of the road, well out of range of Johnson's rifle. The pair riding to the east disappeared into the mouth of a ravine, leaving only a telltale cloud of spiraling dust.

"We gotta keep movin'," Johnson said, watching the second pair of riders cross gentle hills westward. "If them two was only a little closer . . ."

Keeping their horses in a steady trot, he and Johnson moved north toward dancing heat waves. Off in the distance, Crow thought he could see a line of darker green that might be the Rio Grande, although he knew it could be an illusion created by the heat from sun-baked ground. He dared not hope they were only a few miles from the river. There had been enough mistakes made lately founded on reckless hopes, wild dreams.

The first roaring gun blast came from the west. A puff of gun smoke accompanied the report of a rifle near the top of a rocky knob. The horse Johnson was riding squealed and shied sideways; then it collapsed underneath him, legs churning, bawling with pain and fear. Johnson jumped from the saddle as Crow was hauling back on Dixie's reins.

Another shot boomed from the outcrop. The scream of lead on the fly whizzed past Crow's cheek, and he could feel its hot breath before he could settle his gray and drop to the ground. The wounded horse whickered pitifully a few feet away, struggling to regain its feet while Crow knelt in one of the wagon ruts to take aim with his Winchester.

Johnson fired first. The heavy thud of his rifle briefly drowned out the cries of the wounded animal. The mixed scent of gun smoke and blood reached Crow's nostrils just as he sighted in on the shape of a man's head at the top of the knob. He fired and felt the shock against his shoulder, heard the noise of the gun and flinched slightly when it startled him. His heart was racing when he ejected the spent shell and chambered another.

A gun thundered from the south. Zambrano and his lone *pistolero* came charging along the road in a cloud of chalky dust. They were still out of range for the Winchester; thus Crow took aim at the rock again and waited as the horses fidgeted on either side of him, frightened by the loud explosions around them.

"Get off the road!" Johnson shouted, running toward a giant cholla plant beside the trail. "Bring them hosses!"

It was the only sensible thing, and Crow had been blinded to it by the suddenness of the attack. He lowered his rifle quickly and seized the horses' reins. Stumbling over a rock, he led the geldings into the brush as two gunshots blasted from the hill. Something whacked dully into the cantle of Johnson's saddle, tearing off a plug of oiled leather, and the sound made the roan lunge forward, almost knocking Crow to the ground.

Zambrano and the lone gunman continued at a hard gallop along the road, spurring their horses relentlessly. Crow wheeled around and brought the rifle to his shoulder, trying to steady his sights on Zambrano's chest. At two hundred yards he squeezed the trigger. The Winchester jumped and spat flame, emitting a roar which brought a momentary ringing to his right ear.

Blinking, Crow saw Zambrano's horse swerve off the road with its rider still in the saddle. "Missed the son of a bitch," he whispered angrily, levering a fresh round.

The *pistolero* followed Zambrano out of sight before Crow could get off another shot. Then a sound behind him took his attention from the trail. Running feet moved through the cholla spines and yucca. Johnson was nowhere in sight.

He could hear horses galloping near the spot where Zambrano had disappeared and whirled around to face the oncoming riders, at the same time puzzled by Johnson's departure on foot. Now he was alone to battle the pair of charging Mexicans, and there were four more scattered around him someplace, probably advancing on him even now. "This is it," he told himself, trembling with rage and fear as he brought the rifle to his shoulder. "This is where I buy myself a pine box . . ."

The shape of a rider passed between some low mesquite trees; then the *pistolero* charged through the slender limbs, his horse in an all-out run toward Crow. With less than fifty yards between them, Crow took hurried aim just as a pistol cracked in the rider's fist. A bullet struck the cholla plant beside Crow, shredding one of the spikes. Crow steadied the Winchester and nudged the trigger gently when the Mexican was almost on top of him.

A pair of eyes below the brim of a sombrero rounded. An instant later, the man appeared to have been caught by a mighty gust of wind. He flew from the saddle with a cry caught in his throat and tumbled to the ground, bouncing, sliding across an open stretch while lying on his back, arms and legs flopping uselessly until his slide ended a few feet from the spot where Crow was standing. Blood pumped from a hole in the Mexican's neck, he clawed for the wound feebly with both hands, making a gurgling sound.

Another horse raced among the trees farther to the left, a fast-moving shadow, a mere outline. Crow levered a cartridge and swung the gun toward the spot, leading the figure only slightly before pulling the trigger. The concussion from the mouth of the Winchester hurt Crow's ears. A tree limb swayed in the mesquites, and then the rider was gone, hoofbeats pounding away in a different direction.

"You're a smart bastard, Zambrano," Crow hissed, clenching his teeth fiercely, pumping another shell into place. "You make damn sure you never show yourself—let the others take all the chances."

A sudden burst of distant gunfire made Crow glance over his shoulder. Three, four, then five shots rang out near the rocky knob. "Pistols," Crow muttered. "Wonder if they just got Lee."

From a slightly different spot a gun cracked once. Blinded by brush, Crow could only guess what was happening. The Mexican lying near his feet started to choke violently, kicking his legs back and forth, rattling his spurs against the caliche hardpan. One look told Crow the man was dying. A pool of blood the size of a saddle blanket encircled the man's head and chest, turning milky where it mingled with the pale yellow soil.

The sound of hoofbeats faded. A silence blanketed the hills and ravines. For a time Crow stood motionless, crouched down with his rifle cocked and ready. The *pistolero* stopped thrashing back and forth beside the cholla. His knees sagged; then his hands relaxed around his throat, and the blood stopped running from his wound.

Crow felt his heart throbbing inside his chest. Beads of sweat clung to his face. His shirt was plastered to his skin, and his legs were weak. The horses calmed and lowered their heads when there were no more gunshots.

A lone pistol shot banged from the north, this time much farther away. "Where's Lee?" he asked himself in a soft, hoarse voice.

Soon the waiting took its toll on Crow's nerves. He led the horses forward very slowly, keeping to the cover of brush wherever he could, staying wide of the road, sweeping his surroundings with cautious glances before moving to the next clump of thorny plants. The locusts chirped from all sides, blocking out the faint noises a man would make if he approached stealthily on foot from another direction. He knew he could be walking into a trap, and still he continued northward, wondering about Johnson and the *pistoleros* hidden among the rocks atop the knob.

At last he could see the outcrop when he came to an opening in the brush. Here he waited, examining every shadow, covering the open spot with the muzzle of his rifle. The silence had begun to bother him. Where were the others? What had happened to Lee?

Something moved on the far side of the clearing, the shape of a man on foot creeping slowly through the brush. Crow aimed for the figure and held his breath, listening to the drumming of his heart.

His arms relaxed when he saw Johnson step to the edge of the clearing. An unconscious smile crossed his face briefly. "Over here," he said, starting forward with the horses.

They met in the middle of the clearing.

"What happened?" Crow asked quietly, still keeping an eye on the brush.

"I got two of 'em," Johnson replied, taking his horse's reins. "Winged another one, I think. He was holdin' his arm when he rode off."

"I got one more," Crow said, "but I missed another chance to shoot Zambrano. He's a smart son of bitch. Hardly ever shows himself."

"Let's get out of here," Johnson said. "It can't be far to that river . . ."

When they were mounted, Crow remembered an unfinished bit of business. "I'll ride back a ways. That horse needs to be put out of its misery."

"Damned if that don't beat all, Jim Ed. There's a whole handful of mean *hombres* tryin' to kill us, an' all you can think about is hosses."

Chapter 23

Riding cautiously, guns resting across the pommel of their saddles, they kept their horses at a walk. The sun hovered above the horizon, emblazoning the sky with the colors of sunset. As they crested a hill, the Rio Grande lay before them, winding its way across a broad, hilly plain. The road turned east, toward Nuevo Laredo, but Crow knew he would not follow it now. He was headed home.

"Looks like we scared 'em off," Crow said quietly, swiveling his head back and forth nervously.

"I wouldn't count on it jus' yet," Johnson warned, sweeping his eyes over the hills in the same fashion as Crow. "We got a ways to go afore you make it across, an' there ain't nothin' to keep Zambrano from followin' you into Texas, soon as you're all by your lonesome."

Crow hadn't considered going the rest of the way to Carrizo Springs alone. One man on a winded horse would make easy prey for three armed bandits. "I sorta hoped you'd come along, Lee. We've come this far together."

Johnson gave him a look. "Have you forgotten there's

a price on my head over yonder? My momma didn't raise no fool. I ain't plumb crazy."

"I'd guarantee your safety. You'd have my word that nobody'd lay a hand on you. Soon as this money is safe in the vault at the bank, I'll ride back with you."

"Wasn't part of the deal we made, lawman."

"I know. But I'm asking anyway. You've earned your share of the reward. I reckon I'm asking as a friend."

"We ain't friends, Sheriff Crow. I don't make friends outta lawmen. Soon as we strike that river, I'm headed back to Nuevo Laredo. But if you took the notion, you could ride down there with me, I suppose. Don't see what it would hurt. We stay on the Mexican side, where the law can't touch me. That way there'd still be two of us watchin' the money."

The idea of riding alone through the darkness didn't sit well in Crow's brain. "It makes more sense, staying together. Zambrano could be watching us now, waiting for his chance."

Their water-starved horses caught wind of the river's scent and pricked up their ears. Dixie struck a jog trot. The roan hurried its pace as they began a gradual descent to the riverbank, leaving the road where it swung eastward. Willows and cottonwood trees grew along the bank, widely scattered, leaving few places to hide for a bushwhacker. When Crow saw the river up close, less than two hundred yards away, he took a final look over his shoulder and found the hills empty. "We're gonna make it, Lee," he said, allowing himself to relax a little. "Damned if it don't look like we're gonna make it after all."

Johnson grunted, looking back, frowning. "Me, I'd have bet my share of that reward ol' Zambrano wouldn't have given up so easy. There's still three of them an' jus' the two of us. I figured he'd still like the odds."

"Maybe he knew he was whipped. When you snuck up on them and cut down with your pistol, it scared the other two. And you said one of them was wounded in the arm—"

With the words no more than out of Crow's mouth, a gunshot roared from beside the trunk of a willow tree. Something struck Crow's left shoulder with sledge-hammer force, and he went spinning out of the saddle, twisting like a child's top. The rifle flew from his hands. White-hot pain shot through his arm and chest. Dixie bolted away as he was falling; he heard himself cry out, and it was as if someone else made the sound, someone far away.

He collapsed on the ground, the force of impact driving the air from his lungs. Somewhere above him a gun blasted; then the rattle of gunfire exploded from every direction. A frightened horse whickered. Pounding hoof-beats moved away. Despite the terrible pain shooting through him, a single thought invaded his half-conscious brain: he'd almost made it back with the money, and now it was gone, lost to a surprise attack on the banks of the Rio Grande. His friends, the citizens of Carrizo Springs, had lost everything a second time, a second time they would never know about if he died here today.

It was as if something suddenly snapped inside his head. He heard himself roar, and at the same time, he was scrambling to his feet, clawing for his pistol. His pain was miraculously gone in an instant. In its place, he felt blind rage, hatred for the bandits who had changed his life so completely. He had been a man of peace for so long that the new emotion was strange, not a part of him he knew or understood. With his hand clamped around the butt of his Colt, he took off in a stumbling run toward the trees at the edge of the river with the sound of gunshots ringing all around him.

A gun blasted from the riverbank; he saw the bright muzzle flash and heard the explosion. A tiny voice inside his head told him to turn and run the other way, yet a more powerful emotion held him on course toward the willow, an anger beyond anything he had ever known before, a tidal wave of seething rage that drove him onward, toward the willow tree, as fast as he could run.

A man swung around the tree trunk with a gun in his fist. A shot bellowed as Crow was trying to right himself from a near fall over something hidden in the riverbank grass. A voice he did not recognize as his own shrieked wildly; then his finger began to jerk the Colt's trigger as rapidly as he could pull it. Shots banged from his gun in quick succession and still he ran toward the shadowy shape below the tree, shouting, screaming until he was sure his lungs would burst. He gave no thought to dying now. All that mattered was killing the man who stood before him, even if it would be the last thing he did before another bullet struck him down.

The gun clicked on a spent shell. His boot toe caught in the grass, and he fell forward, never taking his eyes from his target while he was falling. The man who stood beside the tree took a step closer, and Crow cried out in frustration, despair, knowing he had missed with all six bullets. Death was certain, for now his gun was empty. He landed on his chest and groaned, blinking, watching the bushwhacker come toward him to finish the kill.

Suddenly, the man's legs buckled. He went down on his knees and dropped his gun to clutch his chest. *"Bastardo!"*

a deep voice cried; then the bushwhacker slumped to the ground.

A gray fog swept around Crow's head, clouding his vision. He fought it until he felt himself slipping away into the mist. Then all was black around him. There was the sensation that he was floating, as though someone carried him. He wondered if he were truly dead now, beginning the journey to the great unknown.

Strange dreams. Meaningless images drifting about in a half-dark world. Faces he did not recognize. Voices that spoke jibberish, nonsensical sounds, murmurs. Weightlessness, as if he had no body, no arms or legs, nothing. He was truly afraid of this dark, eerie place, wherever it was. His thoughts wandered and would not focus. He felt no pain. It seemed as though he was adrift atop an inky sea, sometimes swirling about in eddies or sluggish whirlpools. Where was he?

The sensation of movement ceased, and now he lay still in the darkness. This was surely what it was like to die.

A face appeared before him. For a time he stared at it, a man's face he knew he should recognize. Features were familiar, yet the name and any connection to this man escaped him. As his eyes focused, he discovered he was lying in a room on a soft bed covered with a linen sheet. A lantern burned on a nearby table.

"Where am I?" he heard himself ask, trying to clear cobwebs from his brain.

"You're in Laredo now. Take it easy, Jim Ed. You lost a hell of a lot of blood."

He tried to remember and couldn't, his mind a blank. How had he gotten here? And what was it the man said about blood? "I feel real weak. For the life of me I can't recall your name."

The man grinned. "It's the laudanum. Doc gave you a big dose before he took the bullet out, an' the nurse keeps givin' you more every so often, when she can wake you up an' get you to swallow. No sense lyin' to you about it . . . you're in pretty bad shape, but the doc says there's a fifty-fifty chance you'll pull through. I told him you were always a tough ol' bastard ever since I've known you."

"I still can't remember . . ."

"I'm Clint Sikes. If you wasn't half-drunk on that stuff, you'd know me right off."

Suddenly, events came back to Crow in a rush. He recalled the ambush at the river, the bullet that struck his shoulder and his reckless charge toward the blazing guns. The abrupt awakening left him silent for a time while he sifted back through his recollections. "They were waiting for us at the river. We thought we'd scared them off." He swallowed when talking made his throat dry. "The money. We got it back, only I reckon we lost it again when they jumped us at the Rio Grande."

"The money's here. Six bank bags full of paper money. I havn't counted it yet, but what there is, is safe in the vault down at the Cattlemans Bank."

"How did it get here? I . . . don't understand."

"That negro shootist brought you and the money to my office early one mornin'. Lee Johnson, the feller I told you about over in Nuevo Laredo before you left with the other two. Johnson told me the bounty hunters are both dead."

"Where's Lee? I need to talk to him. Find out what happened and how he got me here. We were jumped at the crossing below Carrizo. I blacked out after I caught the bullet. I don't remember a damn thing." A dull pain was awakening in his left side now, spreading down his arm and across his ribs.

"I tossed Johnson in jail. Got the drop on him when he rode up to the office with you tied over your saddle. He didn't put up much of a fight. He knows he's a wanted man. I can't figure why he'd cross the river with you an' all that cash money. If he was smart, he'd have left you for dead an' ridden off with the bags."

Hearing Johnson's fate, Crow raised his head off the pillow to look Clint Sikes in the eye. "You gotta let him go, Clint. He saved my life. You can't simply lock him up like that, not after all he's done." His head fell back when the pain sharpened in his side. "I gave him my word that he'd be safe on this side of the river until we got the money stored. You gotta let him go, Clint, and that's all there is to it."

Sikes frowned. "I'd be breakin' the law myself if I did that. He's a professional killer, Jim Ed, with a reward offered for his arrest by the sheriff down in Brenham. I already sent a wire down there, tellin' them I've got him locked up. It's too late to do anything about that telegram."

Crow's eyes were riveted on Clint's face. "I gave my word. There has to be some way to let him go free."

A woman in a floor-length gingham dress entered the room. She wore her hair in a tight bun, and when she found the two men talking, she scowled and patted the knot in her tresses. "I see he's awake. Time for more of your medicine, Sheriff Crow, and it's also time for your company to leave. You need rest."

Sikes got up from his chair beside the bed, making the

rawhide bindings squeak. "I'll come see you tomorrow," he said as he turned for the door.

"Wait a minute, Clint. You gotta promise me you'll do something about Lee. I can't let it end this way. I owe him too much."

"I won't break the law, Jim Ed. We'll talk about it tomorrow, when you're feelin' stronger." He clumped out of the room and closed the door behind him before Crow could offer any more objections.

"I'm Miss Higgins," the woman said, bringing a small lavender bottle from the table. "Open wide and I'll give you this laudanum. Then, if you're up to it, I'll bring you some chicken broth later tonight. The best way to get your strength back is to eat something."

Crow hadn't been listening while the woman poured medicine into a spoon. His thoughts were on Lee Johnson down at the Laredo city jail, and a broken promise he'd made to the man who had saved his life on two occasions. He knew he couldn't allow Clint Sikes to turn Johnson over to the Brenham authorities. There had to be a way to have him set free.

He took the spoonful of laudanum and made a face. "Worst tasting stuff on earth," he said bitterly.

"It will soothe away the pain. Now close your eyes and rest while I'm warming a bowl of broth downstairs. I'll bring it up later on, after you've slept some."

He wondered if he could sleep at all with Lee Johnson on his conscience.

Chapter 24

A burning fever came and went. Sometimes he was sweating; other times he felt a chill. For a day and part of the night he lay in this sweltering room, beset by bouts of fever and pain from his damaged shoulder. The doctor came twice, a morning call and late evening again to examine his wound. Nurse Higgins changed his bandages and gave him laudanum. Other times he rested and stared out a window watching the sky brighten, then darken with night. All the while, when he was conscious, he thought about Lee Johnson and the deadly gun battle on the banks of the Rio Grande. Crow remembered very little of it. He kept wondering how Johnson had escaped the fusillade of bullets coming from the trees, how he had been able to hang on to the money, why he'd cared enough to tie Crow over a saddle to see him safely to a Laredo doctor, a trip that had cost him his freedom when he'd ridden into Texas. Johnson had known the risks crossing the river, and he'd taken them anyway. Now he was in jail, because he'd tried to save another man's life. Jailing Johnson was an intolerable act, but certainly within the law. Clint Sikes hadn't come to see him all day, and Crow suspected the worst, that Clint refused to set the gunman free, no matter what guarantees Crow had given him.

It had been dark for four or five hours when he heard footsteps on the stairs. Crow turned his head to the door and waited. The doorknob twisted. With the lantern turned down low, he had difficulty at first seeing who came into the room.

"You look more dead than alive," Johnson said, edging away from the door.

"How did you get out of jail?"

"Seems the door to my cell got left unlocked when they brung me my supper. My hoss was tied in the alley. Somebody wanted me out of jail . . . can't figure exactly who, but it don't matter."

"It matters to me. I gave you my word that you'd be safe on this side of the river until the money was locked away. Sheriff Sikes wired the authorities in Brenham, so you'd better clear out of here as quick as you can."

"I'm goin'. Jus' came by to see how you was doin' afore I crossed over. It's late, so nobody saw me come up here."

"How did you get away from the ambush? When I got shot, there was lead flying all over the place . . ."

"You dropped one of 'em with that mule-headed charge to the tree. I got one more with a lucky shot, I reckon. One got away, took off like his britches was on fire. It was Zambrano. I loaded you on the back of your hoss and brung you here. Had you figured for a dead man, the way you looked. Couldn't hardly tell you was breathin' at all 'til we got here."

"That's when Clint arrested you . . ."

Johnson nodded once. "I took a chance. Appeared it

was a bad gamble, until tonight, when that door got left unlocked."

"It's Clint's way of helping me keep my word to you."

"I took my part of the money out of one of them bags, so it'll be short when you count it."

"I owe you more than money, Lee. I'll never be able to repay you for what you've done."

"I'd best be goin', afore that sheriff changes his mind." Johnson walked over to the bed. He took Crow's right hand and shook it gently. "I told you the other day we wasn't friends, that I didn't make no friend out of a lawman. Maybe I've changed my mind. You've got guts, Jim Ed Crow. There's times when you ain't real careful, but nobody'll ever say you're short on guts."

"Thanks," Crow said as Johnson dropped his hand and turned for the door. "Good luck to you . . ."

The gunman walked out. Crow listen to his boots on the stairs.

The trip home in Alfredo Garcia's wagon was a painful affair, wheels jolting over bumps in the road, a spring-loaded seat without much spring to it. Tinker sat beside him, asking all sorts of questions about the gunfight in Hidalgo and the ride ahead of Zambrano and his men. The money remained in the bank vault in Laredo, until Harriet Sims could be told the Dimmit County Bank had most of its assets again; thus banking business could be resumed. Dixie was tied to the back of the wagon, looking better after two weeks of good grain and hay at the livery stable in Laredo.

"They've planned a little celebration for you when we get back to town," Tinker said. "Rosa Mora has fixed a bunch of tamales an' beans. *Pan dulce*, too, all different kinds, an' some flan custard with carmel on top. Anna Bustamante baked a bunch of cakes. Alice Evans made damn near a thousand cookies. Everybody is gonna turn out to welcome you home."

"Rosa Mora's tamales give me the bellyache. So do her beans. She puts too damn much pepper in 'em to suit me. I'll be awake all night, but I reckon I'll eat 'em anyway."

"The whole town is mighty grateful, Jim Ed, for what you done to save their money. Sure wish I coulda gone with you down there."

"Be glad you didn't. I was lucky to get out with my skin. If it hadn't been for Lee Johnson . . ."

The wagon crested a hill overlooking Carrizo Springs. In the distance, Crow could see scores of people gathered in the streets to greet his arrival.

Tinker pointed ahead. "Ain't hardly a soul who didn't come to town to welcome you back."

The wagon jolted over a rock. Crow winced; then he put on his best Sunday smile. "I'll be glad to see everybody again. There was a time or two when I figured I wouldn't."

"Appears I had that darkie guessed wrong," Tinker said as he slapped the reins over the mules' rumps to hurry them downhill. "I'd have nearly swore he'd be the one to double-cross you. He had that look about him, like he couldn't be trusted."

"Hard to judge men by the way they look," Crow replied as the wagon bumped and rattled past the town cemetery. He let his gaze wander over the mounds of fresh earth, four with grave markers bearing names of the deceased, seven more with simple wooden crosses, the bandits killed during the robbery. It struck Crow then just how many lives had been lost because of those bags of money, for the tally had grown much higher down in Mexico. He'd come within a whisker of losing his own life over the money. It had been spared by the actions of an unlikely guardian, a killer with a price on his head.

Remembering Lee Johnson, Crow looked south to the horizon. Somewhere below the Rio Grande in Mexico, he had a friend to whom he owed everything. It was doubtful they would ever meet again.

The wagon rolled into the outskirts of Carrizo Springs, past the huts of Pedro Garza and his cousins, the simple homes of his many friends here. When he looked ahead, he saw dozens of faces he recognized. Everyone was smiling and waving at him. Some shouted greetings before the wagon came to a halt. He raised his good arm to wave back, feeling better than he could ever remember.

He spied Rosa Mora at the edge of the crowd. "Fetch me a big plate of those tamales, Rosa. Pile the beans on, too. I've been thinking about some good home cooking all the way over from Laredo. Can't say as I've ever been quite so hungry."